HITTIN' LICKS FOR THE HOLIDAY

NEW YORK

FRESHH MONEYY

URBAN AINT DEAD

URBAN AINT DEAD
P.O Box 448
Maybrook, NY 12543

All rights reserved. Published by URBAN AINT DEAD Publications.

Cover Design: P Wise / The Wise Services

Edited By: Shawna Brim / Ladies Of Lit

Contact Publisher at www.urbanaintdead.com

Email: urbanaintdead@gmail.com

Print ISBN: 979-8-9906748-8-2

STAY UP TO DATE

To stay up to date on new releases, plus get information on contests, sneak peeks and more,

Click the link below...
https://mailchi.mp/6d21003686d1/subscribe

Scan the QR Code below to listen to the Soundtracks/Singles of some of your favorite U.A.D titles:

Don't have Spotify or Apple Music?
No Sweat!
Visit your choice streaming platform and search URBAN AINT DEAD.

Currently on lock serving a bid?
JPay, iHeartRadio, WHATEVER!
We got you covered.
Simply log into your facility's kiosk or tablet, go to music and search URBAN AINT DEAD.

URBAN AINT DEAD

Like & Follow us on social media:

FB - URBAN AINT DEAD

IG: @urbanaintdead

Tik Tok - @urbanaintdead

Submission Guidelines

Submit the first three chapters of your completed manuscript
to urbanaintdead@gmail.com, subject line: Your book's title.
The manuscript must be in a .doc file and sent as an
attachment. The document should be in Times New Roman,
double-spaced, and in size 12 font. Also, provide your synopsis
and full contact information. If sending multiple submissions,
they must each be in a separate email. Have a story but no way
to submit it electronically? You can still submit to URBAN AINT
DEAD. Send in the first three chapters, written or typed, of your
completed manuscript to:

URBAN AINT DEAD
P.O Box 448
Maybrook, NY 12543

DO NOT send original manuscript. Must be a duplicate.
Provide your synopsis and a cover letter containing your full
contact information.
Thanks for considering URBAN AINT DEAD.

PROLOGUE

Method Man featuring Mary J. Blige's *All I Need* crooned through the car speaker as Shawn sat back in the passenger seat of the white Hellcat silently. His left hand laid on his wife's thick thigh as he listened to her snap her fingers and sing along. He stared out the window at the snow that fell from the sky and the Christmas decorations adorning every house and business they drove past. The sight caused his insides to burn with anger still in disbelief of what had happened the previous day. His jaw clenched, and his heart raced in his chest. He couldn't wait to catch up with his cousin.

This was Shawn's first Christmas home after a decade behind prison walls, his first as a married man with little ones who he could play Santa Claus for. His heart was supposed to be warm with pride and joy. A part of it was, but the feeling was shaded by the murderous rage and stress consuming his thoughts. He didn't know how he was going to make this holiday an enjoyable one, and he had yet to come up with a way to break the news to his wife.

Awkwardness had never accompanied silence between the couple, but as DJ stopped at a red light, she could tell there was a lot more to her husband's quietness than just basking in the moment. She looked over at her husband —_caramel skin that she loved to taste, a full beard she loved to pull, and a bald head she loved to palm while her legs rested on his broad shoulders. He was tatted up and well groomed. No lie, she loved every inch of his 5'11", one hundred seventy pounds solid build, but her favorite part of him was his perfect smile. If she knew anything, it was him, and it was like DJ had x-ray vision the way she could see Shawn's mind running faster than Usain Bolt.

"You're in your head," she spoke, her raspy voice pulling his attention as she turned off the music. "What's wrong, baby?"

"Nothing, beautiful," he replied and mentally kicked himself in the ass.

DJ wasn't just his wife; the thirty-three-year-old Latina was his twin, confidant, and righthand woman. She knew him better than he knew himself and knew his nothing response usually meant a lot. Shawn leaned over and kissed her pretty lips as he grabbed her chin and looked into her beautiful eyes.

"Just thinking about how lucky I am to have your pretty ass." And he was.

DJ stood 5'2", one hundred sixty pounds of ass and thighs. Her skin was pale and blemish free, perfect for the passion marks he loved to leave on her body, and decorated with many tattoos. Her long, brown hair cascaded down her back, and she always smelled edible. Her eyes were the prettiest he had ever seen, and they enamored every time she looked at him, but she was more than just a baddie. DJ was highly intelligent, nurturing, and evasive as fuck. She completed him. DJ blushed and smirked. Her husband showered her with compliments daily, and they were cherished, each liquefying her insides, but she wasn't easily distracted.

"Uh huh, real cute, but tell me what's wrong, why you're in your head," she pressed as she stared into his eyes.

He broke eye contact, and DJ knew it was bad. Shawn sighed as he sat back, resting his head on the peanut butter leather headrest. He played with his full beard as he looked forward, mentally preparing himself for the disappointment, anger, and sadness he was about to cause her. DJ drove, and Shawn decided the direct approach was best. He had never lied to her, and he wouldn't start now.

"I lost the stash money." He clenched his teeth as he delivered the bad news.

He shook his head, disappointed at himself. There were two weeks before their first Christmas as a family, and he had lost the twenty-eight thousand they had tucked away. DJ's face twisted in contempt as she registered his words.

"Wait. what? How did you do that?" she questioned, flustered.

She turned on a side block and pulled over. There was no way she heard what she thought she heard. His tone was too serious for it to be a joke, and she wanted to cry at that moment. The loss of the money was only half of the reason. The hurt came from her husband making moves without her, most likely because it was an illegal one he had no business doing. During the beginning of their relationship, they had individually lost it all; then along the way, together, they had accumulated everything that they now had —_two cars, a three-bedroom apartment, and the twenty-eight thousand dollars that was now gone. DJ looked over at Shawn in disbelief. They had come a long way together, and their struggle and climb further cemented their relationship, so the hurt overweighted the anger. *How could he leave me in the dark?* she thought sadly.

"I had got next to Leigh, was supposed to be buying a brick," Shawn said honestly. "I already had the sales lined up and would of made a honeybun by New Year's, but the nigga got me. Sold me a fucking kilo of nothing." He bit into his inner jaw as he thought back to the discovery. "I'm gonna…"

"Not to cut you off," DJ interrupted midsentence, "but I thought we was done with all of that. How we go from book deal, clothing line, dealer's license, to drugs? Like you ain't just come home. Make that make sense."

"We got shit to do. We got plans right now. Book deal, clothing line, dealer's license isn't an income. It's a process. Twenty-eight and the wait wasn't gonna get us where we wanna go. I needed motion, so I could buy ya the house you want," Shawn argued.

DJ shook her head before placing her face in her hands and leaning down against the steering wheel.

"Oh, my God," she murmured in distress.

She knew that Shawn was so used to the fast, illegal money that the patience required would be hard for him to possess.

"Our plan is to be a family and be happy. The house could wait. You gave me your word that you would stay legit, baby. We're good. All I needed and wanted for Christmas is you and the kids. That's it," DJ stated emotionally, eyes misting. "That twenty-eight could of held us down, or you could of flipped it legally."

Shawn sighed in exasperation. He was going to kill his cousin. "I'mma get the money back."

DJ heard it in his voice. It was like she could now read minds. "You're not killing anybody," she told him as she sat up and faced him. His silence confirmed that it was what he had been thinking. "Hello." DJ waited until he looked at her. "I'm not playing. You can't do that."

"I could do that. Shit is easy," he quipped stubbornly. "I'ma get our shit back. The kids got a list of shit they want. You want a house."

"Okay, but I rather our family be broke than broken. I'm..." DJ paused, not wanting to add fuel to the fire. "I'm not trying to lose you."

They sat back as silence took over, both deep in thought, trying to figure out what to say and what to do next. DJ knew, even in extremis, her husband was going to make it happen for them. She loved him for that, but she needed him to know it wasn't all about that. Nothing was worth him going back to prison and losing their family. They had made it through hell and high water, breakable situations, and then some to get here. Now they were here, and DJ wasn't trying to repeat the obstacles. She cleared her throat before speaking.

"What do you want to do now?" she asked.

DJ knew Shawn wouldn't take the L on the chin, especially since he was adamant about giving them a good Christmas. As much as she didn't want him to take the risk, she was going to have his back.

"One move, what is it?"

Shawn stared out the window as he digested her words, thoughts processing they had too much going right now to fuck it up doing wrong, but his stubbornness and family desires trumped all logic. They were down, and the pocket money they had wasn't enough to do anything. Fuck it, sometimes you had to do bad to live good, and he was going to make it worth it.

"I'm not fucking with drugs, and I don't take from people." He paused before continuing. "I'ma hit a bank," Shawn stated.

It was a crazy idea, one he used to envision, one that would financially secure them if done dexterously. DJ's eyes went wide as she watched his facial expression. She had never seen him more serious. Her heartbeat raced in fear, and her nipples hardened in excitement. This husband of hers was like no other. She turned toward the steering wheel and put the car in drive.

"You're my husband, so I got your back."

Shawn was confused.

"What you mean by that?"

DJ sat, quiet for a second. "I'ma ride with you, one move. I guess we're gonna rob a bank."

"*They ain't see potential in me, girl, but you see it. If it's me and you against the world, then so be it...*"-Jay-Z

Jay-Z featuring Beyoncé —_03' Bonnie & Clyde
"Mamis a rider, and I'm a roller. Put us together, how they gonna stop both of us?"

"Fuck you mean it's fake?" Shawn pressed the Spanish tester. "You ain't even tried it." He pointed out angrily.

He had just come from buying what was supposed to be a kilo of cocaine from his cousin, Leigh. The twenty-eight thousand dollars Shawn had given him in cash was authentic. The brick better had been too.

"Shit ain't fake" he barked.

Pito raised his hands in surrender.

"I'll tell you truth. I can tell real coco. This shit is baking soda and another things, not what you give me before," he told Shawn as he touched the white, powdery substance and rubbed his fingers together. "They do good job making it look real but no real."

Beep! Beep! Beep!

The honking of the horns from the cars behind him broke Shawn out of his daze, bringing him back to the present. The realization that his cousin had got him had him hotter than lava, and the only reason Leigh would live to see the upcoming holidays was because of DJ. But as Shawn drove, everything in him wanted to hunt Leigh down and murder him. He couldn't place all blame on Leigh though. He knew he had to take accountability for the loss as well. Shawn had been chilling, home for six months, and focused on legitimate businesses. The books he had penned during his incarceration had taken off, his clothing line was due to be released soon, and he had many more blueprints to pursue. While he was focusing on being the breadwinner, his wife was focusing on building her career, and overall, everything was bliss in their relationship and household. His cupidity and ambition had forced him to bet big, and now, he was reaping the consequences. Life was life'ing.

As he drove, he reflected on the past two days and his wife's demeaner. DJ was resilient and forgiving, but he could feel the disappointment, anger, and hurt oozing out her pores. Then, the kids' excitement for the holidays was causing his guilt to triple in size. If it was up to him, he would of ran into a bank days ago and rolled the dice, but DJ made him promise he wouldn't. Things had to be done strategically, the bank had to be chosen carefully, thoroughly cased out, and the getaway had to be smooth. Shawn laughed as he thought back to how DJ had elucidated.

"Let me find out she been studying how to do a bank heist," he said to himself as he parked across the street from his desti-nation. "Let's see how I'm gonna do this..."

Shawn walked in the apartment, closed the door behind him, and removed his constructs. He was exhausted and starving after running around all day. He removed his coat then walked through the quiet house and stopped by his stepson's room. He walked in, chuckling at Abel's wild sleeping position, then leaned down and kissed his forehead. Abel was the coolest eight-year-old Shawn had ever met and one third of his motivation. After walking out, he stopped by Amber's room. The five-year-old was his joy. They'd just connected, and Shawn loved her like she was his own. He looked over at the Christmas wish list on her nightstand and picked it up. Nothing was going to stop him from getting every toy, mythical creature, and candy bar she was demanding from Santa with her spoiled ass. Shawn kissed her forehead before walking out. He stood outside her door, his heart heavy and conflicted. He couldn't afford to not do something, and he couldn't afford to get caught doing anything. Those two innocent souls depended on him to be their day and night and to make this Christmas better than the last. He wouldn't fail in any way. He approached the master bedroom and paused. An argument was on the horizon because, after some thought, he came to the conclusion that there was no way he was allowing DJ to participate in the bank burglary. Her safety and freedom meant more to him than his own, and he wouldn't be able to live with himself if anything happened to her, but like him, she was stubborn as a mothafucker and would protest until he gave in. Only this time, he wasn't giving in.

"Stubborn, light skin mothafucker," he mumbled as he pushed open the door.

The room was dark, but the light from the hallway illuminated enough for him to see DJ laid on their queen-sized platform bed, facing the wall, headphones in her ears.

Shawn closed the door behind him and stripped down to his boxer briefs as he made his way over. He climbed up into the bed, pulling her into his body so that her ass pressed against his manhood. Shawn wrapped his arm around her and kissed her neck. They laid silently for a while, both their minds consumed with thoughts of everything that was going on. Shawn knew she was mad at him, and he had no choice but to respect it. Shit, he was mad at himself. As far as feelings, they were definitely on the same page of the same book. The problems were clear to see; however, the solution was difficult to comprehend. He pulled her headphone out of her ears.

"I know you're mad at me." He spoke softly, the proximity of his voice sending tingles up her spine, but fuck that, she was mad.

"I am," DJ admitted, "but we're here now. It is what it is." DJ had thought it through and accepted what was to come.

It was wild, it was extreme, but it was ensured that they would never need to result to any illegal activity ever again.

"You're not doing the heist with me," Shawn declared.

He felt her go stiff and prepared himself for World War III. DJ raised her head to look back at him with a raised eyebrow and piercing eyes he was glad he couldn't see in the dark. She knew eventually he would come to that decision, but the truth was that DJ was standing on hers. They said beside every great man was an amazing woman who made him the best version of himself. DJ wasn't chancing him doing it alone or trusting anyone to have his back. That was her job, her vows, and she would stand true to them.

"Yes, I am." She enunciated.

Shawn shook his head. Her little, light skin, thick ass was about to piss him off.

"You're not. You got too much to lose. The kids, school..."

"So do you," DJ countered irritably. She hated that he didn't give himself enough credit. "Everything I have to lose, so do you." Shawn shook his head.

"I could holla at…"

"Nobody." She cut him off. "I always tell you to keep your moves to yourself! People pocket watch. They envy and look at your cousin." She pointed out, brutally honest. "You can't trust nobody else but me, you know, that same way I could only trust and count on you."

"Bro, I got a plan. I could do it. I fucked up, not you," Shawn argued, but he couldn't deny that she was speaking nothing but the truth.

"Baby, but we're one," DJ reminded him. "I gotta be at your side where I'm meant to be," she stated. "I spent the day thinking about it and hearing the kids say what they want for Christmas. I thought about our house, our plans. I want us to move forward and not ever have to result to this or anything illegal ever again, so I made peace with it. We do it right, and our lives will never be the same."

Shawn sighed. Again, DJ spoke facts he couldn't argue with. She was the only one he knew would never betray him, the one who would watch his back and remain by his side. He would go harder and be smarter with her there with him. Fucking this up was not an option.

"I sat in front of a few banks, and I wrote down the ones that seem like it wouldn't be so many obstacles, the ones I feel like I could hit by myself," Shawn explained. "So, if you were by my side, shit would be even easier. I'm telling you now, we're gonna do this, but if I even think shit is going wrong, I would kill everybody and die just to make sure you make it home to the kids."

"We're both gonna make it home," DJ said as she held his

face in her hands. "We're gonna live this whole lifetime together and the next."

Shawn kissed her before holding her tight as she laid her head on his chest. He meant every word he said, and at this point, he could only pray that this lick brought joy and not sorrow to the holidays.

———

Shawn knocked on the apartment door and stood to the side, out of view of the peephole. He waited patiently, quietly praying that Leigh would open the door. He had promised DJ that he wouldn't but figured if he did maybe he could retrieve most of their money back and fuck Leigh up in the process. DJ was too dedicated, and that didn't sit well with Shawn. A man was supposed to provide, protect, and make sacrifices for his family. Shawn wouldn't hesitate to do so, but his wife wasn't supposed to be part of the equation. DJ was supposed to nurture, soothe, and sit pretty. That was their roles to keep their family balanced and happy, but with DJ being involved in these extreme measures, she was tipping the Libra scales like a motherfucker. The money that would be obtained from a successful bank burglary was definitely enviable, but to keep his wife safe and secure, Shawn was going to try Leigh first. He wouldn't try to kill him — anymore stains on his soul and DJ wouldn't take it lightly — but he was going to hurt Leigh bad.

Shawn could hear sounds coming from the other side of the door then the scrap of the deadbolts being unlocked before the door swung open. He immediately pushed his way in and wrapped his hand around a petite female's neck, slamming her against the wall opposite of the front door. Her eyes widened in fear as Shawn kicked the door closed behind him and looked down the narrow hallway toward the bedroom.

"Where's Leigh?" he asked through clenched teeth as he turned the lock on the door.

Shameeka shook her head frantically, her body paralyzed in fear. "I don't... don't know," she stammered.

Shameeka knew Shawn and had heard the stories; boy wasn't one to play with. The anger in his eyes spoke volumes, but she was unaware of these violations.

"I... I been calling him. He's not answering his phone," she informed him honestly.

"I look stupid? Where..."

The banging on the door echoed through the apartment, and Shawn applied pressure to her neck as he leaned closer.

"Be quiet or I'ma break your fucking neck," he whispered into her ear before pulling her with him until he could look out the peephole. His forehead creased in frustration and confusion. He let out a forceful breath as he unlocked the door and opened it.

"What did I tell you?" DJ barged in and barked at Shawn.

She paused at the sight of his hand clutching Shameeka's throat. She shut the door behind her and folded her arms under her ample breasts.

"You just so fucking stubborn, and you don't listen."

Shawn roughly pushed Shameeka toward the living room and flung her onto the couch. "Not right now," he replied to DJ, and he looked down to Shameeka.

"Where the fuck is Leigh?" he asked her again.

"I don't know," Shameeka responded, on the verge of tears. "I been hitting him up for the last two days, and he don't respond"

"You're in his crib," Shawn pointed out, growing tired of her acting dumfounded.

Shameeka's face displayed confusion.

"This is my crib," she corrected. "He just stayed here from time to time. He came over a few days ago, took my new bank card, and now he's M.I.A." She shook her head in displeasure. "I don't know where he's at."

It was obvious that the twenty-eight thousand wasn't the only lick Leigh had hit. Apparently to Leigh, 'tis was the season to be grimy.

"So, he got you for your account." DJ stated the obvious. "He's a real dick. Try to call him again, and I'm telling you now, bitch, if you're lying, I'ma let my husband break your fucking face," DJ threatened as she pointed a finger in Shameeka's face. Shawn looked on silently, turned on by his wife's aggression, trying to contain his smirk.

"My phone is in my room." At that moment, hatred grew in Shameeka's heart for Leigh. "I have nothing to do with what he has going; he played me too," she expressed to DJ, who was clearly now in control.

It was like Shameeka now feared DJ more than she feared Shawn. Shawn headed to her room to get her phone, found it, then returned and handed it to her. Shameeka tried Leigh three times, all ending in the same result. Voicemail.

"I told you."

Shawn wiped a hand down his face and punched the wall. He had hoped for a result that would make the bank heist unnecessary. He looked over at DJ and wanted to choke her ass. He loved his wife, but she was making moves difficult to execute.

"We were never here," he told Shameeka. The threat was clear as plastic.

He grabbed DJ's arm and got her out the door then hurried down the stairs and stopped by his whip.

"Who told you to follow me here?" he drilled her. "What if shit got crazy?"

"Exactly why I came," DJ shot back. "You told me you wouldn't step foot in Brooklyn, so when I see your location..."

"Bro, you bugging for real." He interrupted her before calming himself.

Yeah, they bickered and debated, but this wasn't what they did. Shawn didn't raise his voice at her, and she didn't defy him. Leigh had caused more harm than just financially.

"Beautiful, I'ma get us right, but I can't have you do this shit with me. Shit is fucking with my head."

"Big ass head." DJ sucked her teeth and looked away. "You about to do whatever you have to do to provide for our family, and I'm doing what I gotta do to support my husband. That's how it's supposed to go." She stepped as close as possible, looking up at him. "It shouldn't fuck with your head. From day one, it's been us against the world."

"She would do anything necessary for him, and I would do anything necessary for her, so don't let the unnecessary occur..."-Jay-Z

F abolous featuring NeYo - *Make Me Better*
"Your boy a good look, but she my better half..."
Fabolous

DJ sat in class, her eyes on the Sociology paper in front of her, but her mind was miles away. Every second of her day was consumed with thoughts of the lick she had agreed to. Not only had she agreed to allow her husband to commit a felony, but she had agreed to participate. Her love for him was unconditional, and her devotion to her family knew no limits. The way she figured was that she would be there to keep him strategic. She would provide the balance needed to keep everything under control in such a risky situation, and she knew he would move smarter to not jeopardize her freedom or safety. DJ smirked in awe at her husband, a man who loved his family so much that he would go to the greatest lengths to put a smile on their faces. She couldn't stay mad at him, no matter how hard she tried to be.

The class was dismissed, and DJ hurried out. It was her final day before the holiday break, and while everybody was rushing out in pursuit of a relaxing holiday, she was in pursuit of a life changing experience. DJ walked to her car, got in, and slammed her door shut. Tomorrow would bring change. There was just no telling if it would be for the better or worse. She tapped her hand on the steering wheel as she weighted the pros and cons. There were more pros, but they weren't as significant as the cons. She had put in time, effort, and patience to finally have Shawn home with her where he was supposed to be. The circumstances had been challenging, and they had succeeded, but a repeat wasn't an option. The heist would happen the following day, and DJ would make sure they both made it home safe and sound. It was all or nothing.

————

Shawn paced back-and-forth, strategizing the perfect plan. This was reality, nothing like the movies. There was no actors, no cut or action. There were no rehearsals, so there was no room for error. If the smallest detail was altered, they would face great consequences. Well, Shawn would because he was going to get his wife back home at all costs. He had chosen a bank wisely. Everything checked out and made for a potential success. As long as they stuck to the plan, Christmas would be spent lovely. Shawn and DJ used to speak on how their first Christmas and New Year would be spent, but they couldn't even fathom the thought of this. Shawn had to chuckle. His wife was different, a down ass bitch for sure, and he had known that from the start. DJ did things for him that he couldn't believe she did, and he would reciprocate for the rest of his life. Shawn knew that he had almost blown it the day before. He couldn't lie to himself. If Leigh had been present and even a dollar was spent, he would have murdered him with no hesitation. Shit, he was a second away from taking his anger out on Shameeka. DJ had pulled up at the perfect time and saved lives.

"Superwoman," Shawn said out loud, thinking about his wife. He owed her the world, and the money from the bank heist was going to help him give it to her.

———

"You got it?" Shawn asked DJ after going over the plan for the umpteenth time. There was no room for error. Everything had to be precise if they were going to pull this thing off. He watched DJ as she pulled joggers over her leggings and marveled at her calmness. Shawn had been on edge since they had agreed to go through with it, while DJ had been more cool. The past four days had been dedicated to the bank heist. They scouted multiple banks through the day then laid up and strategized through the night. Every other second was spent with the kids, savoring the interaction and praying everything went well. One lick to hit to bring cheers to the holidays.

"Yes, baby. I understand," DJ responded before pulling the turtleneck over her head.

She tucked her ponytail inside and walked over to Shawn as he sat at the edge of the bed, gloves on his hands, thoroughly inspecting the two 9 mm Lugers with a seventeen-round magazine and a double barrel shotgun. The guns was necessary for their plan, but DJ prayed they wouldn't have to squeeze a trigger. That was the one part that made her hesitate, but it wasn't enough to discourage her. She ran her fingers through Shawn's full beard before tugging on it and causing him to stand in front of her. She brought his face close, resting his forehead against hers as his hands slid around her small waist and rested on her ass, pulling her closer.

"We got this. I got you, and I know you will always make sure I'm safe."

The way DJ looked at him, with so much faith and confidence in his ability, made Shawn feel invincible. Since the beginning of their relationship, she had always been the realest on his team, and her commitment to this brazen mission was further proof of how devoted she was.

"Listen," Shawn said as he placed a hand on the back of her neck, "I will die for you, and I will kill for you with no hesitation. Same thing goes for the kids. I'ma do whatever it takes to make sure ya always happy." There was so much passion and sincerity in his words that DJ knew it was the truth.

"We got this," she repeated, fighting back emotions. "We gonna come back home... pick the kids up from Mommy's, and then I'ma cook some tacos," she told him. "Then we gonna lay in bed and you gonna eat my coochie while I count the money." Shawn laughed before kissing his wife.

"Let's go hit this lick."

An hour later, they were parking across the street from a TD bank by Canarsie in Brooklyn. Shawn cut the engine and grabbed the shotgun from between his seat, placing it in his joggers, as DJ tucked the 9 mm in her purse. The white wig, makeup, and glasses concealed her identity, while Shawn wore a Covid mask and shades to conceal his. Once they got to the entrance, the ski mask was rolled down their faces, the guns were drawn, and Shawn rushed in, sprinting directly to the counter where only two bank tellers stood. "Don't move," he ordered as he pointed the shotgun in their direction and grabbed the one customer by the back of his neck, pinning him to the counter.

DJ rushed in a second later, turning to the right, aiming a gun at the one guard and the manager who sat at a desk, caught by surprise. They had noticed that this TD branch didn't have much traffic or employees, and it was perfect for first timers.

"Come lay on the floor. On your stomachs. You move wrong, I shoot," DJ demanded and watched as they quickly complied. She removed the guard's gun and tucked it in her waistband as she watched over them and periodically looked toward the entrance.

"Both of ya come out here," Shawn instructed the bank tellers before directing them and the man to the ground. He then looked over at DJ and nodded toward the counter. As she sprang into action, hitting the registers and filling her purse with the cash, Shawn kept his eyes and gun on the occupants on the ground. They had agreed on a two-minute window and were down to thirty seconds.

"Come on," Shawn whispered as he began to sweat.

DJ hurried through the three registers then ran to the manager's cube where a safe sat and attempted to open it.

"What's the combination?" Shawn asked as he pressed the barrel to the manager's head.

"5... 30... 24," the manager called out, clearly scared and unwilling to lose his life over money that was insured. DJ opened the safe and began stuffing the money in her purse.

"Let's go." She heard Shawn tell her as she grabbed a stack that felt a bit heavier. She tossed it back inside, figuring it was a dye pack, and closed the safe. She hurried out the bank as Shawn backed out until they were outside. They tucked the guns and walked toward the car, hopping in and pulling out into traffic. They drove a few blocks then swiftly pulled over and got out the Nissan Altima that Shawn had rented using a fake name on Craigslist. They walked casually for two blocks until they turned on a quiet block that he had parked on. Shawn took their guns and stashed them along with the money in the groceries that sat in his trunk as DJ got in the backseat. He slammed the trunk closed and hopped in, removing the Covid mask and shades.

"Here." He passed them to DJ as he pulled off.

They drove in silence, both their hearts beating uncontrollably and their eyes constantly surveying their surroundings. Shawn stopped near a dumpster, and DJ threw the bag containing their disguises and clothes inside. Then, they drove home with smiles that couldn't be contained.

———

"Oh, wait. I want this one too!" Amber squealed as she pressed her finger to the screen of the MacBook, causing Shawn to laugh. She grabbed her pencil and paper and began writing down the unicorn playhouse, another gift on her list to Santa, another toy Shawn was going to make sure was under their tree on Christmas morning. Abel joined in, adding every PlayStation game that they scrolled by, and Shawn was mentally adding it to his cart. The heist had been a success, and the Citizen app announced that there were no suspects, stroking Shawn's ego as a feeling of triumph coursed through his body. They had picked up the kids, and DJ had made tacos before retreating to the bedroom as Shawn sat on the couch with the kids, looking online at toys, games, and clothes.

"Do you think Santa is going to get me all my toys?" Amber asked as she looked from her list to Shawn, her light eyes hopeful.

"Only if you not annoying," Abel answered in his teasing, older brother, provoking way.

Shawn laughed and watched as they went back-and-forth. Abel liked to start Amber up, but Amber was a demon. The little girl turned up something fierce, and Shawn found it amusing. The money wasn't worth the risk of losing these moments. He thought back to when he was locked up. Back then, he was just a voice on the phone for them, but to them, his voice delivered a presence that was significant in their everyday life. The two kids had motivated him to be a better man, and although he knew his presence outweighed material things, he would rob a million banks to put a smile on their faces. And not only for the holidays —_every single day of their lives. "How 'bout a house? Ya told Santa what house ya want?"

"We have a house," Amber stated, confusion displayed on her face.

"Yeah." Abel agreed with his sister. "We have a home here with our family."

Shawn nodded at their response. His family. He owed them for embracing him into their clan and giving him the role of provider and protector. He wasn't going to fail them.

"Our family is gonna have everything we want. I'ma give ya the world." After looking at more gifts and reading them bedtime stories, Shawn made his way into the master bedroom where DJ had been holed up. Shawn pushed open the door and stopped mid-step at the sight before him. He was speechless and instantly aroused as *On The Way* by Jhené Aiko featuring Mila J played.

*"I got you on my mind. I touch myself just thinkin about you and
What that mouth do, yeah
When it come down, oh
Lick it up, suck It up, vacuum..."*

The sight of DJ in her deep burgundy, lace lingerie instantly made Shawn's dick jump. The silk, red robe was wrapping paper for his laced gift. As she locked eyes with Shawn, she slowly removed her robe, letting it drop to the ground. He was scanning her voluptuous body. The wine-colored laced bra that cupped her 36-DDD breasts and matching panties that hugged her hips just right, it all sat perfectly on her soft beige skin. Her small waist was accompanied with a silk and lace, burgundy garter belt that aligned perfectly in the middle of her thick thighs.

"I missed you, wanted to show you how much," DJ stated softly.

"Show me, beautiful," Shawn said as he bit his bottom lip.

Shawn's alluring stare made her panties soaked. She could see the passion and desire burning through his eyes. DJ knew he was a natural freak. The anticipation made her yearn for him more because she knew he matched her level of nasty.

"You're mine?" she said provocatively

"Yes, this is all yours," Shawn said firmly as he stripped to his Calvin Klein boxer briefs. DJ bit her bottom lip as she grabbed his hand and sat him on the black, suede ottoman, removing his manhood from his briefs. She got on her knees, grabbing his shaft, looking at him with her seductive gaze.

"This is my dick, Daddy?"

"Ssss, mmm... Yes, baby," he said as he breathed heavily.

Her mouth gripped around his head like a vase; the suction

made chills dress his body. As he looked down, he was hypnotized by her eyes as he watched the passion burn in hers. She sucked his head slowly, coating it with her slippery salvia. He sat up and grabbed her hair as she bit her lip, meeting his eyes with her sexual rage gaze.

"Who am I?" Shawn said firmly.

DJ didn't answer. She loved to provoke him to be slightly aggressive.

"Hmm, oh, you're trying to play... Who am I?" He grabbed her hair a bit tighter.

"Mmm, Daddy..." she said as he smirked in pleasure.

"Stick your tongue out," Shawn stated sternly.

DJ stuck her tongue out while he grabbed his dick then smacked it on the middle, making light wet smacking noises.

"Fuck my mouth, Daddy," she stated as the saliva dripped down her chin.

Without hesitation, he stuffed her mouth with his throbbing erection, taking his time with slow and long strokes. The deeper in her throat he reached, the more his manhood emerged in saliva.

"Bust it open, put his face in it (ooh). He ain't done 'til I say finish. Booty clappin' from the back shots."

Shawn grabbed DJ's chin. Guiding her to get up, they met, kissing passionately, tongues dancing in sync. DJ moved away as his tongue followed. She sucked on it and released it to grab and bite his bottom lip.

"You're something else," Shawn stated humorously.

"For you," she replied as she got on all fours, spreading her fat ass on the bed. He couldn't help but notice the wet spot on her panties. As DJ took notice to his curious gaze, she turned on her back and spread her legs, giving him a better view of her excitement.

"Na, your sexy ass is really fire," he stated passionately as he made his way to her pink glistening cuntcake. He then ran his finger through her slit as he felt her creamy juices, and he pushed his two fingers inside of her, feeling her tight walls grip his every move. DJ started to breathe heavily and gasped as she watched him kiss her clit.

"Mmmm, baby, I want you now," she stated breathlessly.

Zayn's *Pillow Talk* was now playing.

"No, you made me ask you twice earlier," Shawn stated sternly.

He looked from her eyes, down to her ample breasts, to where her panties were pulled to the side, displaying her drenched pussy. His fingers slowly moved in and out, causing sound effects to sound off through their bedroom.

"Come on..." DJ whined as she followed his eyes.

The sight of his fingers coated in her essence, plunging inside of her repeatedly, had her near climax. She watched as he removed his fingers then brought them to his mouth as they locked eyes. He sucked his fingers as he gripped his erection with his other hand, drawing DJ's attention. Her righthand man was ready for action, but she knew her husband loved to tease and dominate in bed. Fortunately, DJ knew how to make him lose self-control. She wiggled out of her panties and threw them at his face playfully as she spread her legs wide. DJ open palm slapped her pussy, a moan escaping her pretty lips, and the act caused Shawn's eyes to burn with desire. She repeated the motion, delivering slap after slap as her clit throbbed and juices leaked down her ass crack. Shawn bit his bottom lip and exhaled sharply. "I'm horny," DJ stated seductively as she raised her legs back and gripped the back of her knees, spreading herself wide.

"Who am I?" Shawn asked again as he settled between her thighs, aggression evident in his tone.

He gripped his dick in his right hand as he hovered over her, his body covering hers. He slapped her clit with his dick then pressed on it firmly before making circles, spreading her wetness and his precum. DJ's eyes lowered as her forehead pinched, and she bit her lip sexily.

"You Daddy," she said with no hesitation.

She opened her eyes and looked into his submissively. He was Daddy. He was her king, her God. The man of her dreams and love of her life.

"You're trouble." She gasped as he pushed into his safe place. DJ moaned loudly as he stretched her tightness, filling her perfectly and going deep. "You're dangerous," Shawn groaned as her insides gripped him. He pulled out, causing her to cry out in protest, and kissed down her body before leaning in and planting kisses on her southern lips then sucking her clit into his mouth.

He devoured her pussy, feeding his hunger and bringing her to a powerful climax. Her cream oozed out her pussy down to her asshole, and Shawn's tongue mopped it up before kissing up her body, savoring the taste of her flesh, until their lips locked. DJ reached down and gripped his strength, rubbing it along her protruding clit before guiding him inside her sex, his favorite place on Earth. She gasped then let out a loud moan as he stretched her, filling her up, and dived deep. Her pussy gripped him as she gripped the back of his neck.

Shawn stroked out then in as she sucked on his neck then bit him and dug French tips into his back.

"I love you sooo much, Daddy." She moaned as Shawn hit harder. "Fuck! You feel so good," she purred in his ear. "Tell me how good my pussy is."

"You got the best pussy in the world," Shawn groaned as he felt her walls vibrating. "Cum on this dick. This shit belongs to you, sexy. Soak it," he demanded before biting down on her nipple. He felt her cum, and he exploded, burying himself deep in her body. Shawn planted kisses along her chest and neck as she came down from her orgasm, her body tingling and her pussy holding him tight. He pulled out slowly then turned her over before pulling her onto her knees. Shawn grabbed her ass, spreading her cheeks, and pushed in until her big 'ol booty touched his abs, causing moans of pleasure to bounce off the walls as DJ gripped the sheets above her head. Shawn gripped her waist with both hands and went to pound town until she came twice, and his nuts were drained. They laid silently, both satisfied and on a high, unable to resist trading kisses as they cuddled.

"Baby..." DJ started before pulling his bottom lip between her teeth and pulling on it. "I think we should hit another lick..."

"*D*ynamic duo. Batman ... Robin...Whoever don't like it, it's that man's problem..." -Fabolous*

CHAPTER

THREE

Adrenaline rushed through Shawn's body, giving him a natural high. He could see the occupants of the small M&T Bank branch as they stood in line, waiting to be serviced by the Caucasian bank teller. His old age decreased his agility, and the customers were clearly agitated. No guard was present at this bank, and the two surveillance cameras faced the entrance, so once Shawn and DJ took a few steps inside, they would be off camera. Shawn pushed inside the bank with his ski mask already pulled low and his gun hidden behind his back. He moved like a ninja, light on his feet and swiftly, and before they knew what was going on, Shawn was up close and personal. He jumped over the counter and pointed his gun at the bank teller.

"Back up and put your hands behind your head," he ordered then pointed his other pistol at the two customers who looked on, glued to their spots. The manager stepped from the back and froze momentarily at the scene before him. He snapped out of it and began backpedaling but was stopped.

"Uh-uh." He stopped at the feel of the gun pressed to the middle of his back.

He looked back at the woman he had just been attending to in his office. Her black hijab made it impossible to identify her features, and she provided no forms of identification, which was why their short interaction had been cut so short. The manager swallowed the lump in his throat and raised his hands in surrender as she pushed him forward, guiding him where the other hostages were at. DJ removed his phone from his pocket and threw it in the basket with the others that Shawn had confiscated.

"Get the bread," Shawn told her as he held the hostages at gunpoint while they sat behind the counter. DJ opened the register, shaking her head at its near emptiness.

"Where's the money?" she questioned the manager as she removed the shortchange. She pulled open the drawers until she got the one that was locked.

"That's all we have," the manager lied.

"My life isn't worth insured money," the bank teller spoke up. "Just give them the money so we can keep our lives." He removed the keys from his belt and passed them to Shawn, who tossed them to DJ.

"Listen, I'm not going to hurt anyone. I just want the money," Shawn told them, as he heard DJ trying the keys on the locked drawers. DJ found the key and pulled the drawer open, exposing a few stacks of small bills. She quickly stuffed them into her bag, frustrated that no real money was there.

"Got it?" Shawn called out to her. They had been inside for a second too long, and he didn't want to push their luck.

"Not really. Where's the big money?" DJ directed at the manager, growing angrier by the minute. She wasn't taking risks for money that could be spent on one of her Target trips. She wanted enough to financially secure them. Shawn shook his head. They didn't have time to interrogate or investigate. They had to go.

"We done. Time's up," he told her.

He then focused on the hostages.

"Please don't make me hurt ya," he said as he tucked his guns and casually walked out with DJ following close behind. They rushed toward the corner, made a turn, and sprinted toward the stolen car as they took in their surroundings. They jumped in, and DJ wasted no time pulling off. They only drove two blocks before stopping and switching cars. They got in another stolen vehicle and drove a good distance before stopping at a parking lot where they parked and got out. DJ hurried to the passenger side of her Hellcat as Shawn got on the driver's side. They removed their coverings and drove until they located a sewer. DJ opened the passenger door, quickly throwing the clothes in the sewer.

"This was a bullshit lick," she said as she slammed the door shut.

DJ removed the stacks from her purse, shaking her head as she noticed the largest bill had Andrew Jackson on it. She counted up the take before stuffing it back in her purse.

"Seven fucking thousand!" she huffed.

Shawn exhaled in exasperation. Two banks and all they obtained was $17,000. He looked over at DJ. Her beautiful face was knitted in irritation. He had no words to comfort. Shit made no sense. Shawn had expected to be up after one, but for them to have hit two and still have less than they lost was mindboggling.

"We can situate some other shit."

"We can hit a bank that has more money," DJ retorted.

They had come this far, and it wasn't just to come this far. She wasn't stopping until they got enough. She wasn't 50 Cent. It wasn't get rich or die tryin, but it definitely wasn't settling for less than they lost.

Shawn's brow bent as he looked over at her. Yes, his wife really was certified. He didn't know if he created a monster or discovered one, but it was scary to witness. He had to admit that the thrill was exciting... satisfying. It was an aphrodisiac, and DJ must have felt the same way. The sound of her unclicking her seatbelt came seconds before she was on her knees in her seat, leaning over the center console. She urgently fished his erection from its confines, and then he was in her mouth. They both let out sounds of pleasure as DJ sucked and slurped slowly. Shawn pressed down harder on the gas, his speed going from forty-five miles per hour to sixty-five miles per hour as he enjoyed his wife's head game.

At a red light, he ran his fingers through her hair before pushing her head down, instructing her to engulf more of his big dick. DJ moaned and took him in until he was touching the back of her throat. She sucked harder, desperate for his nut. She felt the car pull over, then Shawn placed it in park as he reached over, rolling her tights and panties beneath her ass cheeks. He slapped her ass then gripped it, spreading a cheek as he pushed a finger into her drenched pussy. She was so wet as his fingers plunged inside her love box repeatedly that a squishy, squashy sound filled the car, collaborating with her slurping sounds and moans to make a perfect, most erotic instrumental. Shawn landed a smack on her ass cheeks, an echoing sound resonating. She moaned from deep in her soul, the vibration bringing Shawn undeniable pleasure, so he began landing smack after smack.

Every time his hand met her flesh, her pussy gushed and gripped his fingers hungrily. The pain felt blissful, the pleasure unbearable, and as he stroked the tips of his fingers against her G-spot, DJ squirted like a super soaker. The sight of her wetting up everything and feeling her teeth chomp down on his manhood firmly caused Shawn to bust in her mouth and lean his head against the headrest in pleasure. DJ leaned up after a minute and looked over at her husband. "I couldn't help it," she said factiously, as she grabbed a napkin from the glove compartment and began wiping herself.

"No, that was your way of seducing me to agree," he joked back as she cleaned him up too. "If that happens after every lick, we hittin' one every day," he stated, causing DJ to laugh. Shawn grew quiet and closed his eyes.

"You sure you wanna do this? I'm not. I fear it being three strikes and we out," he stated honestly. Shawn knew that they were beyond lucky. First one was luck; second was a blessing. A third was just pushing it.

"I'm sure," DJ replied with no hesitation. "But we need one worth all of this. A spot that we know we going to leave with at least a hundred thousand."

She knew that the more money than most likely the more risky, but she was confident in their ability. They were calculating; they were chess players. Shit, they were successful bank robbers.

Shawn drove, relieved that they had again pulled off the lick. The money was short —he agreed with her —but to get to the big bag, they would have to get to the vault, which meant they would have to be inside the bank for a longer period of time and increase the risk.

"With great risk come greater reward," Shawn said, remembering a quote he had read somewhere as he stopped at a red light.

"Uh huh," DJ agreed as she leaned toward the window and looked out. She then sat straight up. "That one." She pointed at the Maspeth Federal Savings Bank that stood directly to her right. They watched as a guard carried two large bags from an armored truck into the bank. He then returned only to grab more bags of money. DJ's clit throbbed, and all she could see was dollar signs.

"That's the one we gotta hit."

"*Cause I'm your chick, the Bonnie to your Clyde...*" *-Charli Baltimore*

FOUR

DJ Mustard featuring Roddy Rich —*Ballin*
"Now a nigga can't answer calls cause I'm ballin..." -
Roddy Rich

Leigh immediately tapped on the chicken spot counter as he waited on his cheese fries. He had been moving, hard to reach because he had been up to no good. There was no shame or guilt on his conscious for the shit he had been pulling or who he was pulling them on. He was hitting licks for the holidays and had no picks, friend or foe, family or stranger. Leigh was on some real selfish, slime ball shit.

"Yo, my order ain't ready?" he asked the ock who shook his head no. "How long do it take for some fucking fries?" Leigh grumbled as he focused on his iPhone.

He tapped on the Facebook app and came across a news

report of a bank burglary that had been committed hours prior. He read the post and shook his head in awe.

Whoever hit that shit probably super up, he thought in wonderment.

There were no suspects reported, and the only description was that one was a man, and one was a woman. Leigh thought back to a report on Channel 12 news he had caught just days ago.

"Na, they on some real Bonnie and Clyde shit," he said to himself with a chuckle as he liked the post then reread it. No suspect, no leads, just a flawless heist.

"Shit, they better than the movie, *The Town*," he commented.

Leigh was amazed by the couple but could never be inspired. He preferred to finesse a little differently. A notification popped up from his WhatsApp, a message from the shorty whose house he had left that morning. Leigh didn't even read the message but clicked out the app. Like Shameeka, she was probably hitting him with threats and cursing him out after realizing that as soon as he had withdrawn the $2,400 from her account that he had finessed, he was withdrawing from her life completely. Leigh didn't stop to think about the financial woes of his victims. In his mind, their responsibilities weren't more important than his. He was doing what he had to do like the courageous couple he had just read about. Only if he knew he was the cause of the desperate measures by being the culprit of their desperate times.

His fries were boxed and placed in front of him.

"Finally," Leigh said as he scooped up the bag and headed toward the exit.

He walked out and stood outside. His head was on a swivel,

and for some reason, his gut was screaming for him to take his ass back inside and sit down for a second. He looked across the street at the armored truck unloading money into the Maspeth Federal Savings Bank, and he smiled at the thought of all those dead presidents contained in those bags. His smile dipped instantly as he recognized Shawn's Bentley and could see him sitting in the driver's seat, eyes on the armored truck.

"Oh, shit." Leigh backpaddled inside the chicken spot, his heart beating faster than it ever had and perspiration forming on his brow. He couldn't believe he had been so close to being spotted by Shawn where he would have never expected to see him. Leigh just realized how dangerous he was playing by walking around without a care in the world. He had one more lick cooking up, then he was going to fall back until after the holidays.

———

Shawn chuckled at the kids' excitement as they ran through the toy section in Target, grabbing everything in sight. Him and DJ had decided to treat their family for a job well done. A couple of new toys, clothes shopping, and a nice dinner sounded about right. As Shawn assisted the kids with their toys, DJ went crazy through every other section. His wife was the only person he knew that could splurge thousands in a single trip to Target and still not have everything she wanted. She deserved and earned the right to, so he wasn't complaining.

"Wait. If I got toys now, Santa is still going to bring me presents, right?" Amber asked as they headed toward the register to purchase the items. She clutched her Barbies close to her chest protectively with the meanest mug she could muster plastered on her face. Shawn laughed as he pushed the cart.

"Of course. You deserve it, so you're going to get a lot of presents," he told her.

Shawn stopped behind a brown skin female and her son as they placed their items on the checkout counter. He could overhear the female going back-and-forth with the worker and felt bad. If it was DJ and the kids, the worker would have been dead as soon as he clocked out.

"Ugh. I'm tired," DJ said as she came up behind them with her hands full of a variety of things. "Ya got what ya wanted?" she asked the kids who answered in unison.

DJ's attention was also pulled by the interaction of the female and worker.

"All I'm asking you to do is swipe my card again," the female pleaded while also trying to keep her toddler from running loose. "The card is damaged, but it's money on there," she stated pleadingly.

She had been having one hell of a week, and this was the last thing she needed.

"I tried three times, and it keeps declining," he responded, annoyed. "Apple Pay or something but we too packed for the drama."

"I don't have a phone," the female snapped, embarrassment and irritation coursing through her veins. She was displaying class but was a second away from showing her ass and turning up. She tucked her hair into her skully and removed her glasses.

Shawn shook his head as he peeped the items she was attempting to purchase —_diapers, household appliances, and clothes for her toddler. He looked back at DJ, and she nodded, reading his mind.

"I got it," Shawn interrupted the dispute as he stepped forward. The female looked at him then at DJ, surprised by the act of generosity. Shawn paid for the items, ignoring the woman's protest.

"Oh, my God. Thank you so much." The female repeated to him and DJ as they grabbed their bought items. "I have money on my card, but I need a new bank card. I can pay you back. Just give me your number," she told them. "Once my card is fixed, I'll buy a phone and Apple Pay you."

"It's okay," DJ responded. "You don't got to pay us back."

They had taken so giving a little was a way to balance out the misdeed. Hopefully, the act of altruism sent blessings their way, and the next heist would be as smooth as the others.

"Look at it as an early Christmas present for you and little man," DJ told her as they all got on the elevator and took the ride down to the main floor.

The female continued to express her gratitude. "I really appreciate you so much. I owe ya a big one," she stated, looking at them through lust filled eyes. She had never encountered a more attractive couple. Shawn and DJ complemented each other well, and one couldn't help but to admire the pair. Their generosity and confident aura enhanced their attractiveness. DJ and Shawn caught each other's eye and shared a laugh.

"You never know. One day, we might need you."

———

"There's two security guards. I couldn't see if they carried weapons," DJ informed as she looked at the video she had recorded while parked outside the bank during the beginning of their workday. She squinted her eyes as she rewound to the part when a guard flicked his cigarette and turned to go inside. "Okay. Yeah." She tapped the iPhone screen. "He has a gun."

Shawn looked closely, sizing up both guards. They were both older Caucasians and clearly out of shape. Shawn nodded

"I got them. The camera is over the door, not that far up but out of your reach." He shared what he had learned when he walked inside to inquire about an account. "It sees every angle of the bank."

"I could knock it down with a broom or something," DJ suggested. The last two heists had been rushed, and the two-minute window didn't provide enough time to properly retrieve the cash. This time, they were going for the vault, which required more time. They were going in, and they weren't coming out until they had more money than they had ever had at one time.

"Na. You can't hide a broom." Shawn paused in thought.

He though back to the door. You had to pull it to enter and push to exit, but if something held the handles closed, it was damn near impossible to push or pull.

"A steel pipe." Shawn decided. "You could hide it in your sleeves, smash the camera, then use it to secure the door." He strategized. "I'll take care of the guards."

"Nobody dies." DJ reminded as she looked at him seriously. "We scare them, you apply physical pressure if need be, but nobody dies, baby."

"I already gave you my word on that. I won't do it for no reason but to get you home. I won't hesitate," he told her. "We don't leave unless we have to or until after we get into the vault." His heartbeat increased at the sound of the plan. This was going to be the lick that would change their lives. DJ nodded in agreement. They needed this one last lick to make their holidays blissful for years to come. She hoped things didn't end like the movies when one last score became the last score the person really could ever do.

"*I run up with racks with my queen like London and Nip...*"-
Roddy Rich

CHAPTER

FIVE

2 1 Savage featuring Summer Walker – *Prove It*
"She a dollar way more than a dime..."-21 Savage

Jay-Z and Beyoncé's *Part II (On the Run)* was now playing.

"Who wants that perfect love story anyway, anyway... Cliché, cliché, cliché, cliché. Who wants that hero love that saves the day anyway... Cliché, cliché, cliché, cliché. What about the bad guy goes good, yeah... An innocent love, I'm misunderstood, yeah. Black hourglass, our glass, toast to clichés in a dark past..."

DJ stared at herself in the full-length mirror, her eyes displaying determination. Her eyes took in her appearance — black Adidas track pants, Yeezy 350 sneakers, a black, spandex turtleneck, and black gloves. Shit was about to get dark. She looked at her hair as she tucked the red braids inside the turtleneck. Red was the devil's color, and the one on her shoulder was to blame for her gloze attitude toward another bank burglary. She watched as her husband came up behind her, pressing against her rounded backside and wrapping his arms around her securely. They locked eyes through their reflections and silently stared. Words weren't needed for them to communicate; they understood each other perpetually. At first, DJ felt guilty for convincing her husband that another lick was needed. They had agreed that $9,555 from the first bank and the seven thousand from the second wasn't enough, but their relationship was ambiguous. Shawn could see the fervency in DJ's pretty eyes that reflected his own. More money wasn't needed. It was wanted, and their desire to provide their family with the best while securing their foundation was the motive. A Molotov cocktail of emotion threatened to set the room on fire, but they tucked it deep and kept their minds on perfectly executing the plan.

"You ready to go and get this money, Daddy?" DJ asked as she gave a sexy smirk.

"I can't do it without you." Her confidence in him always made him feel invincible, and this time was no different.

"I got you."

"**B**oy meets girl, girl perfect woman... Girl gets to bustin' before the cops come running uh... Chuck the deuces, chugging D'usse, ugh... Fuck what you say, boys in blue say uh..." -Jay-Z

———

The last two days had been spent on perfecting their plan. They constantly cased the bank, they drove a bunch of different getaway routes, and they went over the plan until it was memorized. They felt like they had it all figured out, and there was nothing left to do but do it. Shawn had a thought of hitting a smaller bank, but DJ didn't want to roll the dice and get the same results. In her opinion, this one was it. She felt it in her gut the moment she had watched them transport the heavy bags stuffed with the money inside of the bank. They needed life changing money, especially when they were taking risks that came with life changing consequences.

They finished getting ready then, hand in hand, made their way out the door. Nobody would have suspected that they were on their way to hit a lick for the books. They wore matching gray sweatsuits over their clothes, and to anybody watching, they were a regular, beautiful couple leaving their home to have a regular day. They got into DJ's Hellcat and sat for a second before pulling away from the curb. Music played low as they drove into Brooklyn and parked by Shawn's mother's house. They got out after Shawn killed the engine and walked inside of his mother's building where a camera pointed toward the entrance. Shawn hurried upstairs and used the spare key to enter the apartment. He took his and DJ's iPhones and tucked them underneath the couch cushion then made his way out. Both of their locations were on, and with the camera showing them enter the building, they had a reliable alibi if things led to that. He descended the stairs and walked toward the back of the building and out the backyard. He climbed over the fence leading to the house across and walked along the side of the building, coming out on the next block. Fortunately, there were no cameras in sight. He strolled over to where DJ stood next to a motorcycle Shawn had purchased months ago. It was a 2014, Ducati Streetfighter with 848 longitudinal, twin 849 CC, all black everything. DJ handed him his helmet, hers already in place, then they climbed on, and Shawn gripped the throttle.

"You ready, my queen?" he asked DJ as she held onto him tight.

DJ nodded her head in excitement.

"I'm ready, my king!" she answered as he took off.

"I don't care if we on the run... Baby, long as I'm next to you... If loving you is a crime, tell me why do I bring out the best in you? I hear sirens when we make love, loud as hell, but they don't know... They nowhere near us. I will hold your heart and your gun. I don't care if they come, no..."

Shawn picked up speed, his adrenaline rushing as he raced toward the money. He knew that there was a possibility that this would be his last ride with his wife, and he accepted that. Shawn would face any and every consequence head on, but his wife was going to make it home with enough money to financially secure their family. These licks during the holiday were becoming an addiction that they couldn't continue to feed. This had to be the last, so he would make sure it was a satisfying one. DJ tightened her grip around her husband's body, wanting to never let go. Their memorable moments played in slow motion before her eyes, and she couldn't help but to say a prayer. DJ wanted to create more. She needed to create more memories with this man who she had met over the phone and instantly connected with. A lifetime was the minimum duration of time she wanted to spend with

Shawn, and she wasn't letting anything or anyone cut it short. DJ wasn't a killer, but for her significant other, she wouldn't hesitate to bust. There was no way she was going home without him.

"I know it's crazy, but they can't take me,.. Now that I found the places that you take... take me... Without you, I got nothing to lose..."

———

Leigh checked the mobile bank app and cursed in frustration, pinching the bridge of his nose. The stimulus check for $11,000 was cooked up to perfection, and with the bank account he had deposited it in, shit should have cleared up with no problems, making funds available for withdrawal, but it wasn't. The balance showed that $11,000 was in the account, but the account was placed on hold. Leigh hoped he didn't fuck up the quick lick by making too many inquiries. The account was a good one, the account owner a friend of a friend who he was zoeing and going ghost on. This would be his last lick, then he would chill and do things he liked to do until the holidays passed, so he couldn't afford for it to get closed. "Fuck that," he huffed as he pushed off the couch and began getting dressed. Walking in was risky but worth the reward, so it was his next option. Leigh quickly dressed and left the motel room he had been at for the past two days. Seeing Shawn had made him move smarter. If Shawn would have spotted him, the repercussions could have been severe, and Leigh wasn't for the physical, so he would avoid it at all costs.

He pulled open the door, inspecting his surroundings before stepping outside. For late December, the weather was unusually warm, and Leigh inhaled the fresh air as he began walking the short distance to the bank. He flipped his Pepsi blue hoodie over his head and kept his fitted cap pulled low as he moved along. Time was of the essence, and Leigh had a pep in his step, wanting the money like a fiend wanted narcotics. He turned the corner onto the block of the bank and could smell the fettuccini as his palms began to itch. It was time to get this money.

———

DJ turned toward Shawn after watching a man enter the bank.

"Okay, that's three people so far," she informed.

They had been watching the doors for the past thirty minutes, counting the people who came and went and checking for any unsuspected mishaps. So far, they'd found none. Shawn nodded as he cocked his gun and tucked it in his waist. They had shed their sweatsuits and left the motorcycle chained up a good distance away then climbed in a stolen Impala. He grabbed the steel pipe and handed it to DJ, observing as she pushed it up her right sleeve. Shawn looked at the time and prepared himself. The plan was to be executed before lunch break to avoid unwanted traffic, which meant they had to go now.

They both looked out at the bank and tried to slow their racing hearts. The Maspeth Savings Bank branch in Queens was the perfect candidate for what they were looking for. The bags of money they watched get transported from the armored truck was still inside. The only obstacles in their way of getting to it was two armed security guards, three bank tellers, one branch manager, three civilians, and one surveillance camera. The element of surprise, along with the two chrome 9mms and a Glock 17, was sure to tip the scale in their favor, and once they got the vault opened and grabbed as much cash as they could, their getaway would be effortless. The plan was to make it back to Shawn's mother's house then to DJ's mother's crib to grab the kids, then they were on the road to a cabin in the Poconos until New Years was over. Shawn grabbed DJ's hand, giving it a reassuring squeeze.

"Let's go, beautiful."

You know you my baby, you know you my twin..." - *Summer Walker*

CHAPTER
SIX

*S*ean Kingston featuring Juelz Santana and The Dey – *There's Nothin'*
"There's no one like you, and there's no one like me, so there's nothing like us..."-Juelz Santana

Bonnie Parker and Clyde Barrow were the most infamous couple in history. From 1932 until 1934, at the height of the Great Depression, the couple committed multiple burglaries, including fifteen banks, helped five convicts escape from prison, and were known for their bloody trail of murder victims, consisting of nine police officers and five citizens. Their run came to an end on May 23, 1934 when, after being betrayed by a friend, they were caught in a roadblock, which resulted in their deaths after attempting to flee. What Shawn and DJ were doing was nowhere on the infamous couple's level, and they had no plans to follow in their footsteps, but the end result could potentially be similar, and that was the couple's fear. They had succeeded in two, but this one would be grandiose.

Shawn leaned over the center console as DJ met him halfway, and they shared a soul stirring, passionate kiss.

"I love you most." Shawn pecked her lips as he held the back of her neck, looking into her beautiful eyes.

"I love you." DJ pecked him then pulled on his bottom lip.

They took deep breaths then climbed out and headed toward the entrance of the Maspeth Federal Savings bank. Shawn moved ahead then lowered his ski mask over his face as he pulled open the door, holding it open as DJ stepped through. DJ rushed in, her ski mask hiding her identity, removed the steel pipe from her sleeve under the camera, then swung like she was hitting a piñata. Shawn removed his two chrome 9mms from his waist as he shot past DJ, rushing toward the guard who was standing by the counter, engaged in a conversation with a customer who wasn't accounted for. The guard was slow to react and found himself at gunpoint. "Don't fucking move," Shawn stated, his baritone commanding authority as he placed one pistol point blank against the guard's head and pointed the other in the direction of the three bank tellers and three citizens.

"Remove his gun with your left hand and throw it toward the entrance," he ordered the female the guard had been speaking to. The woman did as she was told and took a step back, raising her hands in fear. Shawn then directed the bank tellers to move from behind the counter and had all hostages lay face down.

DJ smashed the camera then quickly turned, placing the pipe through the two handles, securing it. She removed the Glock 17 from her waistband and turned in the direction of the customers but quickly focused on the manager and a man who were emerging from an office door. DJ gasped when she recognized the man standing before her dressed in a blue hoodie, Leigh.

"Down," she ordered them, pointing her gun at where she wanted them to lay. Her gut instinct told her things were about to take a turn for the worst at the same time it occurred to her that she didn't see the other security guard. Shawn looked up after stripping the hostages of their phones and displayed a look of malice in his eyes at the sight of Leigh. It took all self-control to not walk over to Leigh and empty the clip in his face. Shawn spotted movement from his peripheral, but before he could turn, all he heard was DJ scream out.

"No!"

BOOM!

The sound of the gun going off echoed through the bank.

DJ had caught the movement of the second security guard just in time. His service pistol was gripped in his palm as he snuck up on Shawn, and DJ didn't hesitate to raise her arm and squeeze the trigger, sending a bullet crashing through the guard's head. His body and gun crashed to the floor right by Shawn's feet, and blood splattered everywhere, causing the hostages to whimper fearfully. Shawn turned toward DJ in bewilderment as he realized he had almost had his head blown off. He picked up the gun and tucked it, thoughts of the repercussions flooding him. He looked down at the hostages, ten in total, and could see the look of fear in their eyes. Shawn moved toward DJ, who still had her smoking gun aimed at the lifeless guard.

"Beautiful," he whispered to her, pulling her attention.

There was fear, shock, and fire in her eyes, and her lips trembled as she stifled her cries. Bile filled the back of her throat, and her stomach felt hollow as she looked back down at the lifeless guard, a pool of blood beneath his head.

"Look at me." He gained her attention. "We're leaving." He decided.

DJ wished she could turn back the hands of time and go back. But she couldn't. Every single step that led them to the present was for a reason.

"He was going to kill you," she spoke just above a whisper as she fought the urge to cry.

She had committed a murder. Caught her first body. Stained her soul with blood. Her hands shook as she gripped the murder weapon. If she hadn't killed the security guard, it would have been her husband laying stiff. She looked into Shawn's eyes and couldn't control the tears that escaped. Her actions weren't done callously; she had done so amorously. DJ could live with that as long as she wasn't living without her husband. The bar had been raised, and she definitely wasn't leaving emptyhanded now.

"We're not leaving until we get the money," she protested.

Shawn blew out a sharp breath. His wife's torment was unbearable; he could see that through her tough exterior. He knew firsthand what committing murder did to a person's mind and soul. Shawn never wanted that for his family, especially not his wife and kids. He pulled her close to his body as he looked over at the hostages. If they were going to keep going, they didn't have much time to waste.

"Okay, beautiful. So, let's..." Shawn stopped midsentence, and his heart skipped a beat.

He felt DJ's body tense, and they both realized a bad situation had just gotten worse...

Flashing red and blue lights, along with sirens, were pulling up outside. It sounded like the entire precinct had arrived at the bank burglary. Shawn shook his head slowly then sprang into action. "Watch them," he told DJ as he moved to close every blind in the bank then bent the pipe to prevent entry. He took printer paper and tape from behind the counter, moving fast to cover the glass of the door, obstructing any view of inside the bank. He made sure there were no entry points or ways to peep in then walked over and powered off every phone confiscated. There was only one way in, one way out, further stacking the deck against them. Shawn had no fucking idea how they were going to make it out of this situation alive and with their freedom.

"Fuck!" he barked before aggressively moving toward the hostages, causing them to scramble away. He grabbed Leigh, lifting him to his feet before hitting him hard across the face with the butt of the gun. Leigh screamed out from the impact as the gun busted his lip, and he fell onto his back. Shawn was relentless, kicking him repeatedly as Leigh balled up, trying to absorb the force of the kicks unsuccessfully.

"Nobody else move!" DJ stated. Her voice was stern, and the hostages looked at her, glued to their spots. Nobody was trying to be her next victim.

"Baby, stop!" she called out to Shawn. "Stop!" DJ knew if her husband lost control, there was going to be more than one corpse close by. She had to bring him back down and balance him out the way only she could. "Baby, I need you to stop. Now."

Shawn stopped mid-kick and backed away, breathing heavily. Leigh had caused the domino effect that brought them to this very moment. Granted, Shawn knew he had no business trying to cop a brick, but Leigh had slimed him with no regard. They said money and blood didn't mix. Leigh was the perfect example why.

"This is your fault," he sneered down at Leigh. "All I was tryna do was flip my money to give my kids everything they wanted and buy my wife a house. You knew that, and you still dead me?" He moved close and kicked Leigh. "You gave me fake fucking work."

Leigh groaned in pain, and tears streamed down his face as he broke down fearfully. He had been confused by the attack at first but learning that it was Shawn had him scared shitless. He couldn't believe how that bitch, karma, had sneaky linked him. Leigh would have never expected to bump into Shawn so soon, especially not as a hostage in a bank burglary that Shawn was committing. "Cuzzo... I'm sorry," he said, blubbering.

"You sorry?" Shawn's face twisted in disgust. Banks had been robbed. Murder had been committed. It was too late for the sorries. DJ moved in front of him, stopping him from causing more harm and slightly calming him. The sound of the bank's landline ringing caused them to hold their breaths. Shawn looked down at his wife, knowing she needed his guidance more than anything.

"I made you a promise, and I will never break my promises to you," he told her. "I'ma get you out of this," he promised her then leaned down and pressed his forehead against hers.

"Get us out of this," DJ responded, her eyes pleading with him. They had made vows... plans together for a myriad of the days that couldn't just come to an end two days before their first Christmas together. There had to be a way out.

"Nobody else can die," she told him as the phone continued to ring.

Shawn began pacing back-and-forth, formulating a plan in his head. He stopped and turned toward the hostages.

"None of ya is gonna get hurt unless ya try something stupid. We just came for the money."

The move wasn't made malignantly, and he needed them to know that.

"Everybody is going home to their families tonight. Just please don't make me have to hurt anybody."

"Just turn yourselves in!" the black as night bank manager spat. "Do all of us that favor."

"Shut up!" a light skin, heavyset bank teller snapped at him. She shook her head and stared a hole through the manager. His Uncle Tom ass knew how to push a person's buttons and would definitely be the one who'd make Shawn kill them all.

Shawn's eyes darkened, and anger fueled him, and before he knew it, his hand was gripping the manager's collar, and he was digging the barrel of his 9mm into his forehead.

"My wife ain't going to jail," he stated firmly. "I will set this whole shit on fire before that ever happens."

He pushed the manager away and stepped back as DJ stood next to him.

"What's your name?" he asked the light skin, heavyset bank teller.

"Carrie."

"I need you to answer the phone and let them know that everybody is okay," Shawn instructed, hoping that would buy him more time to figure something out. The last thing he needed was for the NYPD to become overzealous and blitz the bank. "Let them know that only changes if they come in."

DJ nodded in agreement. "Yeah, let them know that they're responsible for everybody's safety," she instructed Carrie. "If they try anything, then everybody in here is going to die."

. . .

"*This ain't a dream. My shorty is a ten...*"-*Juelz Santana*

SEVEN

il Durk featuring Summer Walker – *Difference Is*
"Don't let her see the other side. I be with them
demons, and the difference is..."-Lil Durk

etective Lori Dominguez was the NYPD's hostage negotiator and had been so for the last five years. Yet this would be the first time her skills would be utilized. The Spanish, thirty-year-old with the slight accent had a lot to prove, and as she awaited an answer, all eyes were on her. The SWAT team posted along the building, waiting on the lieutenant's signal, but the lieutenant was waiting on Dominguez. They had received the call from a security guard who had been using the bathroom when he heard the commotion. After peeking out and discovering the reason, he had quickly called 911 and reported the bank burglary in process. Dominguez had been at her desk, shuffling paperwork, when she heard the news and rushed to her lieutenant's office, practically begging him to allow her to lead. He reluctantly agreed but made it known that he wouldn't be overly patient. Lieutenant Lutrell wanted the hostages safe and the suspect dead or in handcuffs before the New York field office of the Federal Bureaus of Investigation arrived and took over.

"Hello?" Dominguez spoke into the phone when she heard the line connect. She tapped on the desk, pulling an officer's attention and motioning for a pen and pad. "My name is Lori Dominguez, and I am a detective at the 104 Precinct. May I please ask who I am speaking with?" she spoke as she was given a pen and notepad.

"My name is Carrie, and I'm one of the bank tellers." Dominguez wrote notes as she listened. "We're all okay, but that will quickly change if you guys try to gain entry." Carrie relayed the message. "Please don't. Just be patient."

"Carrie, I will do my best to keep everyone out here patient and everyone in there safe. How many safeties am I responsible for, Carrie?" Detective Dominguez needed answers because, at the moment, they really had nothing to work with but an employee list. She held her breath, trying to hear any noise in the background. "I was told that there was a loud blast."

"There was," Carrie confirmed at Shawn's direction. "It's a bunch of us here," she answered vaguely.

"How many burglars? You can just say no when I say the number. One..." The line went dead, and Dominguez shook her head.

"What did she say? What do we have?" Lieutenant Lutrell questioned as he approached.

"Nothing really. Yes, there was a gunshot, but she didn't confirm that anyone was hurt nor did she confirm the number of hostages, and the line went dead when I tried to find out how many suspects," Dominguez informed. Her thoughts ran rampant. She needed to gather intel sooner than soon. She needed to speak to the suspect. Dominguez picked up the phone and called again. "Hello, Carrie?" she asked, happier than a stripper getting hundreds rained down on her. "I just want to help everybody get out the bank safe and sound, but I need to know how I can do that." She held the phone tight against her ear and could hear whispers but couldn't make out a voice or what was being said. "Carrie? Can you help me?"

"We just need you guys to be patient. If you come in, he will kill us," Carrie spoke through the phone. Dominguez wrote on her notepad and held it up to the lieutenant and surrounding detectives. "There's a dead guard, and everyone else is fine."

"Can I speak to him?" Dominguez pushed her luck. If she could get the suspect on the phone, then maybe her skills could convince him to let the hostages go. "With a lifeless body inside, my partners are on edge and anticipating another. We're here to serve and protect. We can't stand by and chance him killing someone else." Dominguez snapped her finger and pointed at the folder containing the employees' information. She went down the list. "Carrie, is Ms. Veronica, Ms. Debra, and Mr. Parrish okay?" Dominguez needed a head count, and if Carrie confirmed, that meant there were at least five inside, the security guard who made the call included. She also needed to find out who was dead.

"Just be patient so he doesn't kill anyone else." Carrie ignored the question then hung up.

"We have to move in," another detective by the name of Fields stated matter-of-factly. "There somebody in there dead," he pointed out, "which means he can't be saved."

Dominguez retorted, "If we go in, he kills another. It's obvious that he's capable." She sighed in frustration as she chewed on the end of her pen. She looked down at the notepad in her hands. One male suspect. One unknown corpse. At least five hostages. "We have to be patient and see what he says." She hoped all went well because lives and her career were on the line.

———

Carrie hung up the phone and looked over at Shawn. Lowkey, she was rooting for the couple as she watched them sympathetically. "Anything else?" Shawn shook his head as he sat on a desk, DJ standing between his legs.

"I appreciate you," he told Carrie then directed her to join the others. Shawn's head was spinning as he slowly drew up a blueprint. He had instructed Carrie on exactly what to say and had created the illusion to the cops that there was only one male suspect, clearing DJ from the burglary and murder. Now, he had to get in the safe then figure out how to get her out undetected. DJ looked up at her husband and shook her head. She knew what he was trying to do and had just done.

"You just don't listen," she told him. Regardless of how he spun it or tried to force her, DJ wasn't walking out alone. She couldn't walk without her backbone. "Either we both stay or we both escape this shit. That's how it's going to go. So, if you want me to get home to our beautiful babies, figure out how to get yourself out too."

"Somebody has to bite this bullet." He shrugged. Shawn felt his chest grow tight because the reality of the situation. Somebody had to be the sacrificed to clear the sin and the family's foundation. Never would Shawn let it be his wife. "I told you from day one I would take a bullet for you, beautiful. There's no way for both of us to make it out." Hurt was evident in his tone, but his pride wouldn't let him show it. As long as DJ made it out, he would accept his demise.

"So, how am I going to make it out?" she asked rhetorically. "Same way I could so could you. There's only one exit."

"I'm going to figure it out," Shawn spoke through clenched teeth. He stood up and walked over to the hostages then grabbed the manager. "Is there any other way out?" he questioned. If there was anyone who knew, it was the bank manager. The manager shook his head.

"Only through the front door," he informed honestly. "There's no other way out," Shawn bit down on his lip in anger. There had to be a way. "I won't tie ya up or make ya uncomfortable, but I need ya to comply. Don't try nothing because it won't work. Do what I say and that's my word. Nobody will get hurt," he spoke to the hostages. "I need you to open the safe," he told the manager.

"You will not get away," the manager stressed. "There's no way out. You're just making it worst."

Shawn couldn't understand the manager. The older man was making it hard to keep his composure. "I don't get it. You're willing to get hurt over money that doesn't belong to you." He shook his head as he pointed the gun at the manager's head. He was done being nice to the man. "Open the fucking safe." He sneered with aggression. If the manager bucked at his demand, Shawn was going to buck rounds and buck his ass down.

"There's two cameras in there," another bank teller blurted out as she looked from Shawn to DJ, who stood close by his side, her gun resting by her thigh. The fair skin, middle aged bank teller, Debra, felt the same way Carrie did. Shawn's demeanor toward them had been inscrutable, but it wasn't minatory. She was also six months pregnant and wasn't willing to take the risk of being hurt by anyone or anything. "And if he starts from the right..."

"What are you doing?!" the manager yelled at her, appalled by her behavior. He was definitely firing her once this was all over.

"If he starts from the right, the vault will sound off and completely lock," she told him.

Shawn nodded, thankful for the information. "Thank you, Debra." He read her name tag then looked down at her baby bump. "You okay?" he asked her, guilt now coursing through him. Debra nodded her head, and Shawn pushed the manager forward.

"All of ya come on... Just walk slowly and into the bathroom," Shawn instructed. With no phones and no windows inside the bathroom, there wasn't anything they could do. He moved a chair in front of the door, jamming it underneath the doorknob, preventing it from being able to turn, then followed the manager toward the vault. He opened every door on their way, finding a mop closet, and grabbed a broom stick. "Open it," he told the manager as they stood in front of the large, steel, fireproof vault. The manager started from the left, punching numbers in until the screen blinked green, and the vault was unlocked. "Where's the cameras?"

"One to the left and one right above the door," the manager informed. He finally realized that his resistance wouldn't dictate anything. He had to do whatever Shawn wanted and hope for the best.

Suddenly, his life meant more than his reputation as a no tolerance bank manager. Shawn pushed him to the side and told DJ to watch him before he rushed in with the broomstick, quickly smashing both surveillance cameras. "Bring him in," he called out to DJ. He flicked on the light, and his eyes went wide as he faced the steel table and discovered bills of different denominations, all banded neatly. It was more cash than he had ever seen in his life. He looked over at DJ, who was glued to her spot, eyes on the piles of money. "How much is here?" Shawn asked the manager. Even before the exact amount was disclosed, he knew it was, without a doubt, life changing money.

"It's one million eight hundred thousand," the manager informed. He had been a bank manager for seven years, a bank teller for seven before that, and could never get used to the sight of so much cold, hard cash at arm's reach. It was like the feeling a recovering crackhead felt in the presence of some crack and a glass pipe. DJ couldn't contain the excitement that warmed her body. Her nipples pebbled, and her pussy grew wet. They needed that money, and she had thoughts of her husband wilding her up on top of it. She stepped to the table and grabbed a stack of bills, thumbing through the dead faces. "Baby..." she said huskily before clearing her throat. "You always said you would give me all of my heart's desires. This is it." She waved her hand in the direction of the money. "I want this, you, and the kids," she stated as she grabbed another stack.

Shawn removed the duffel bag that he had stuffed in his hoodie and began stuffing the money inside. One point eight million was more than enough for DJ and the kids to be financially secured.

"I'ma get you out of here with it," Shawn told her as he continued to stuff the bag. He suddenly stopped at the sound of banging and reached for his gun.

"Stay here," he ordered DJ, but of course she didn't know how to listen.

DJ grabbed the manager by the back of his shirt, using him

as a human shield as she followed behind Shawn to investigate the noise. Shawn's brow bent in confusion when he noticed it was coming from the bathroom he had locked the hostages in. They were trying to gain his attention. Thinking that it could be an orchestrated distraction, Shawn moved cautiously, his gun leading the way, confident with his wife watching his back. He moved the chair then pushed the door open.

"He's catching a seizure!" Carrie yelled out, pointing at the male citizen on the floor convulsing.

Luckily, DJ was very knowledgeable in the medical field.

"Everybody come out and stand by the wall," Shawn instructed as he held his weapon down by his side. Once they were there, he moved to the side, and DJ walked in. He watched as she quickly assisted the man, easing him onto his side. He hoped it wasn't a trick because if it was and his wife was harmed, he was dropping everybody where they stood. DJ kneeled by the man, the heat from the bathroom overwhelming.

"You okay?" Shawn asked her, concerned.

"I'm hot," she replied, looking up at him.

They had been in the bank, under their ski masks, for over an hour, and the feeling was uncomfortable, but to remove the ski mask meant identifying themselves. Leigh knew who they were, but Shawn had decided that no matter how things played out, Leigh wasn't leaving the bank breathing. Then, the idea hit Shawn like a punch from Mike Tyson. It was risky, but they had no other options at this point.

"Take your mask off," Shawn told her, causing DJ to look at him, confused.

"Just trust me, beautiful." DJ followed her husband, removing her mask as he removed his own. Shawn looked at her and smirked, pulling a small smile from her.

"The most beautiful woman I ever seen in my life," he complimented, making her blush as the man gained consciousness. DJ stood and walked over to Shawn.

"You good, man?" The man slowly sat up, shaking the fuzziness and looked over at the couple before nodding.

"Thank you. Thank you so much." Shawn helped him up and allowed him to sit in the chair before turning toward the other hostages. Him and Leigh locked eyes, and Shawn's trigger finger began to itch. The fake ass sympathetic expression on Leigh's face didn't move Shawn at all, but it was definitely going to be used for his benefit.

"I remember both of you," one of the females spoke up. Until that moment, neither Shawn nor DJ recognized her as the female that they had helped buy her items at Target. "My name is Erica. You guys paid for my stuff at Target for me and my son because my card was damaged," she remembered fondly.

Shawn nodded at her and could see how her revelation had caused the other hostages to look at them in a new light, which was exactly what he needed. Shawn would gaslight the people in order for them to persevere, then he would try his luck. To win the war, you had to win the people, and right now, he was at war with New York City Police Department, who were feening to break through the front door.

"I'ma ride for my baby. There ain't nothing I wouldn't do for you. I pull up, won't leave you hanging..."-Summer Walker*

EIGHT

M eek Mill featuring Kehlani – *Ride for You*
"But I'll kill for the love of the love you and I built. It's ride or die still…"-Meek Mill

"N o!" DJ snapped at Shawn as they stood a good distance away from the hostages. Shawn had told her his plan, and there was no denying it was a strategic one, but she was jacking it because it didn't include Shawn making it out with her.

"We already spoke about this." Every time he mentioned her leaving without him, it felt like he was smacking divorce papers on her forehead. There was no way she could agree to allow him to sacrifice himself. Jail or dead, she was not with it. He had to come home with her, not only for her either.

"It's the only option we have, beautiful." Shawn tried to get her to understand. Time wasn't on their side, and it was only a matter of time before the cops outside lost patience and bullied their way through the door. Shit pained him too, but he would take the hurt to ensure that his wife didn't.

"So, pick that phone up and call Amber and Abel," DJ yelled at him emotionally, causing the hostages to stare in their direction. "Abel kept saying he wanna play his new Mortal Kombat game with you, and Amber said she wants you to write her a Christmas bedtime story," DJ spoke as tears now spilled freely down her face.

"And me..." she paused, a lump forming in her throat. DJ had meant to give him some exciting news the day he had first broken that he had lost their stash money. Her news was supposed to change their lives, but his news had become the perfect substitute.

"I'm pregnant." She dropped the bomb as she looked into his eyes. The plan had been to tell him while in the Poconos as a part of his Christmas present, but maybe telling him now would give him more motivation to make it out right along with her. "We're having a baby." She emphasized every word.

Shawn's eyes filled with tears —some of regret, most of joy. He stepped close, placing his hands on her stomach and pressing his forehead against hers. He had wanted this since the first day they met, but now that they were blessed with this addition to their family, they were in a situation that threatened to break up the happy home. Shawn cried along with his wife. He cried because he had fucked up. He cried because he was angry and wanted to murder Leigh. He cried because he had created life with the woman of his dreams.

The hostages looked on, their emotions on display, hearts going out to the couple. Shawn and DJ's love was so passionate, and they were so in tune with each other that they had the type of marriage people inspired to have. For their family, they had risked it all together. How could a person be mad at that?

"We should help them," Erica whispered to Carrie. She had promised them that she would pay them back, and maybe she could.

"I'm game, but there's not much we can do," Carrie whispered back, agreeing with Erica. She stole glances at the rest of the hostages. Her two co-workers, Veronica and Debra, were rooting for the couple as well. So was Pete, the man who DJ had helped when he caught a seizure. The other female civilian had tears in her eyes at the couple's display of affection. A hopeless romantic, Christina was the young woman's name, and she was sure to be on board. Leigh, Earl, the manager, and Thomas, the security guard, were all questionable.

"Those three aren't going to be happy." She nodded toward the three men as she spoke to Erica. Carrie knew that Veronica was close to Thomas, so maybe she could persuade Veronica to convince him, but that still left two.

"Mostly question the manager," Erica responded.

Carrie clearly had some naivete to her because Erica had been watching Shawn all night as he constantly stole glances at Leigh. His eyes said it all. Leigh wasn't leaving this bank; he was leaving this earth. Shawn pulled back and looked down at DJ as he wiped her tears then planted a soft kiss to her lips.

"I'ma get us home," he told her and could see the relief wash over DJ. That quick, he had brainstormed and came up with a plan that could possibly save him too.

"I need ya all to walk into the vault." He turned and spoke to the hostages.

They all stood and did as they were told. Him and DJ followed behind them, and once they were all inside, he pointed to Erica and Carrie.

"Let me talk to ya." He waited for them to walk out before slightly closing the vault and walking a small distance away. If there was one thing Shawn was, it was observant. He didn't miss anything and had peeped the two sharing a hushed conversation and eyeballing the others.

"Ya got an escape plan or something?" DJ looked at them, confused, but stood beside her husband with her poker face on.

"No." Erica answered for them. "I told you I owed ya one. We want to help."

———

Detective Dominguez's jaw dropped when she spotted the FBI heading in her direction. She could smell their arrogance as if it was a strong scented cologne and knew they were about to pull rank and take over her operation. As they neared, the phone rang, and she quickly answered, holding a finger up to the agent as he flashed his credentials.

"Carrie?" she asked eagerly. Her fingers were crossed, and her heart thumped, praying that they gave her something she could use to keep her as the head detective and hostage negotiator on this case. "Carrie, are you there?"

"Hi, Detective Dominguez?" Carrie replied with a question of her own. "He's ready to help you help us because you've kept them patient. But I'm only allowed to talk to you and not the federal agents that just arrived."

Unbeknownst to the detective, Shawn had an iPhone Facetime sitting discreetly in their parked getaway car and was able to have an eye on what was going on. He needed Dominguez to know that they couldn't do any slick shit. He had hoped for the best but always prepared for anything. Dominguez looked around in bewilderment, wondering how he could see them when they had combed every inch of the windows and door, and their view inside was completely obstructed. Dominguez cleared her throat and kept her composure.

"That's no problem, Carrie. How is everybody holding up?" she asked, genuinely concerned.

She ignored the agent that was trying to get her attention and turned away.

"Is there anything I can do for ya? Anyone else hurt?"

"Everybody is doing fine. Hungry but we're unharmed," Carrie told her. Shawn didn't know how long they would be inside, but it would be a few hours longer if he wanted his plan to work, so food was essential, especially with two pregnant women inside.

"Sure, no problem. What would ya like?" Dominguez figured she could get a body count based off how many meals they ordered. But as she jotted down the order, she realized she had to give the suspect some credit; he wasn't stupid.

"How is he ready to help me help you guys, Carrie? While the food is being ordered, can we discuss that?" Dominguez slid the pad to her partner, informing him to place the food order.

"When the food is delivered, he's going to let one hostage go," Carrie said before disconnecting the call.

Dominguez stood silent as she sat the phone down, processing the conversation. The suspect was calculated and a worthy opponent. He had eyes on them, yet they were blind to the intimate details of the situation. Every meal was family sized, so they couldn't get a head count, and he chose to deal with the NYPD and not the Feds, knowing they wouldn't negotiate.

"Dominguez, care to brief? Any updates? Anything?" Lieutenant Lutrell questioned, clearly upset that the FBI had arrived. He needed Dominguez to give him something to rub their noses in. "Anything, Dominguez?" he repeated, hope gleaming in his eyes.

Detective Dominguez nodded as she turned toward them. With the progress she made, the intel she gathered, and a hostage being released, there was no way they could sit her on the bench.

"They will only speak to me," she informed firmly. "Their words, not mine." She couldn't hide the glee in her voice.

"Their? As in more than one? And since when does a criminal make the law?" Federal Agent Sawyer spat in disgust, his nose crinkled.

"The suspect won't speak. He delivers his messages through a bank teller named Carrie Davis," Lieutenant Lutrell answered him.

Dominguez continued.

"He will be releasing a hostage upon the arrival of their food. So, it's needed asap," she stated.

Lieutenant Lutrell smiled proudly at Dominguez, giving her a wink of approval.

"Do we know who the suspect is? Description? Is this Carrie Davis an accomplice?" Agent Sawyer shot his questions rapidly, pissed off to say the least.

"We don't, and she's not." Dominguez kept it brief. "We have no way to get a look inside, but he has eyes on us."

"*T*old you that shit gonna be forever, you gon' remember me..." *-Meek Mill*

Tupac – *Me and My Girlfriend*
*"All I need in this life of sin, is me and my girlfriend...
down to ride till the bloody end..."*

Shawn looked down at the unregistered iPhone he had purchased and watched as the officers began looking around in alarm. He had them thrown off, and it was exactly how he needed them. How could they stop what they didn't see coming? He had come up with a plan, but there was no time to perfect it. There would be hiccups but hopefully not enough to make them inviable. Every step had to be made strategically so that they could make it home in one piece. If things didn't go according to plan, he was going out like Queen Latifah in *Set it Off* so his wife could get low like Jada Pinkett.

"I really do appreciate you," he told Carrie as he hung up the phone and leaned back in the chair. Her comfortability in their presence didn't go unnoticed. It was like she was a part of their team. "You've been helpful. I'm gonna let one person go when the food gets here... You're next up."

"I'm good. I could wait it out," Carrie responded surprisingly. "I don't mind playing secretary." Shawn and DJ shared a look. Neither knew anybody who would volunteer to be a hostage in any situation, but there Carrie was, volunteering to do so. She had been the most frightened when they had first rounded up the hostages. Now, she seemed to be the most supportive. "And I really want you two to make it out okay, especially for ya baby."

Shawn turned to Carrie. "Let me talk to Erica." He waited until she entered the vault before he spoke.

"I don't want to necessarily involve you in anything, but I have more faith in you than them. You out when the food comes in, but I need a favor." Shawn had originally planned to release DJ under guise of her being a hostage, but she was relentless in her protesting; she wasn't walking out unless they were hand in hand.

"Whatever ya need," Erica replied wholeheartedly. In her eyes, they were good people who were in a bad situation and needed some help. When the shoe had been on the other foot, they had assisted with no hesitation or agenda. There was no way she would leave them stuck.

Erica held no fear or animosity toward the couple. Her dark eyes only showed admiration, and that was why she was the next best candidate. Their lives kind of depended on her doing what they were asking her to do. It was a crucial part of the plan, and they couldn't afford for her to fuck it up or switch up once she was out and in the presence of the law. Shawn took his time explaining and repeating every detail until she was able to repeat it to him verbatim. Shawn excused her then sat silently, praying that he wasn't making a mistake. DJ stood between his legs and wrapped her arms around him, laying her head on his shoulder.

"Everything is gonna work out, right?" DJ asked. She needed her husband to confidently assure her. Shawn kissed her forehead

"Have faith in your light skin." DJ had been the one keeping him optimistic throughout the whole ordeal. Now, it was his turn. "All I need you to worry about is how you want me to eat it tonight. From the back? You sitting on my face? What's up?" he joked.

DJ giggled and looked into his eyes. She would follow this man wherever he chose to lead her for the rest of their lives, especially if it came with those incentives. "You're trouble." Shawn pressed his lips to hers, the kiss spilling some of his strength to her and him receiving some motivation from her.

"You're dangerous, beautiful." He kissed her again. Just then, the phone began to ring, no doubt with the call from Detective Dominguez about their food. "You ready to eat?"

———

"Are you crazy? You are not going inside!" Lieutenant Lutrell barked at Detective Dominguez as she pulled her long, black hair into a ponytail. The Feds stood close by, a smug look on their faces as they observed their exchange. They had agreed to give the NYPD one hour to wrap up the heist. After that, they were taking control and doing it their way.

"Dominguez, I'm giving you an order." He lowered his voice so only she could hear him. "The answer is no."

"That I'm asking you not to give me. This was his order, and if we try it any other way, somebody is gonna die. If I walk in between the doors and drop the food off, somebody's life is gonna get saved. How are we debating this right now, sir?" Dominguez looked at him with a curious stare. "Let me save a life," she pleaded.

Dominguez was a cop who had a genuine passion for actually helping people. She naturally felt empathy, so this was important to her. While most cops wanted to be the one who killed the suspect and saved the day and the higher ups wanted the political ratings for solving the case, Dominguez just wanted for everybody else to be safe, the suspect included. She grabbed the bags of KFC as she waited on the lieutenant's response. Lieutenant Lutrell ran a hand through his thinning hair in exasperation before pointing a finger at Detective Dominguez

"Be careful." Dominguez was on the move before he could give a lecture. SWAT members got into position, stepping back a distance at her order as she approached the front of the bank. Dominguez took a deep breath before opening the first set of double doors and stepping inside.

The silence was loud as she stared ahead at the second set of doors that were completely covered up. Her heart raced uncontrollably as she waited. Two minutes, that was how much time Lieutenant Lutrell had agreed to wait before he gave the order for SWAT to go in for her. Dominguez stepped closer but came to a halt when the door was pushed opened. A brown skinned, petite female slightly stepped out, and Dominguez could see the gun pointed at the female from behind the closed door.

"Hi, I'm Detective Lori Dominguez. Are you okay?" she asked as she took a step closer and held her arms out to pass the food. The clock was ticking, and she didn't want time to run out. Erica nodded frankly, playing a role of traumatized hostage. She grabbed the food from Dominguez and stepped back.

"My superiors allowed me to come alone but on a two-minute countdown. If I don't step outside within that time, they're going to react. Please, I don't want things done that way," she spoke as she looked at her watch. She had less than a minute left and didn't want to walk out emptyhanded. "You agreed to let a hostage go." Her heart raced faster and sweat formed above her brow. Thirty seconds left. "Please, just one and we could work on the others. I'm willing to be patient, but please, let's not let them overreact. Let me walk out in the next..." she looked down at her watch again, "ten seconds with a hostage." The door opened up, and Erica stepped in view, her butt pushing the door as she dragged the lifeless security guard out.

The door swung closed, and Dominguez could hear it being secured just as the front two was yanked opened.

"Wait! Drop your weapons! Stand down!" she yelled, jumping in front of Erica after SWAT members held their guns up. "I have a hostage. We're coming out," she told them as she helped Erica bring the body out. The SWAT members quickly assisted as Dominguez guided Erica toward a waiting ambulance while Erica clenched on her arm.

"You're safe now. You're okay."

———

Shawn and DJ looked down at the iPhone in his hand, watching as Erica was escorted from the ambulance to the area where Detective Dominguez was set up. Shawn was anxious, unsure of how Erica would move forward. The ball was in her court and out of their hands. He had always been a good judge of character, but none was ever trusted with such an important task that determined his and DJ's lives.

"Even if that bitch gets cold feet, I'ma get us home," he said before turning to DJ and pecking her lips. He sounded more confident than he felt. Truth was, there was no Plan B for them to make it out. If Erica didn't pull through for them, he was forcing DJ out as the next hostage and shooting it out with the law. Shawn had been to prison where he had spent the majority of his life. DJ had dedicated time and energy riding it out with him. That experience wasn't one he wanted either to repeat, so it was what it was; he was being sent to the morgue, not to bookings.

"I'ma go get the pregnant woman," he told DJ as he hopped off the desk and walked into the vault. What he saw was exactly what he wanted to witness. Every hostage sat around the money, eating their food and discussing what they would do with the amount of money that sat in front of them. Shawn cleared his throat, pulling their attention. He then pointed at Debra.

"You're leaving.""

Debra slowly stood, saying her goodbyes and grabbing her belongings before making her way out the vault. Shawn grabbed the duffle bag full of money and dragged it out behind her, closing the vault behind him.

"Debra, I need you to do me a favor," he told her as DJ stepped by the door that Debra would soon be walking out of. "Trust me. It's worth it."

———

etective Dominguez observed Erica as she answered the other detective's questions, and her heart went out to the twenty-four-year-old single mother.

"Can you remember anything else about him?" she asked, wrapping up the questioning.

She was sure that Erica just wanted to get home to her family, and after the morning's events, Dominguez understood. Erica shook her head; she had answered enough questions and was ready to get away from the pigs. Dominguez called over a uniformed officer and directed him to take Erica home. She waited until Erica was secured in the backseat of the patrol car before looking down at the notes she had scribbled down from the information Erica had provided.

"I really believe..." Her words were interrupted by pandemonium.

Dominguez and her partner shot to their feet as the SWAT team began moving in.

"Woah, woah, wait!" Dominguez yelled as she sprinted over.

The front door of the bank was being pushed opened slowly, causing the cops to panic, not knowing what to expect. Dominguez unholstered her service pistol as she neared the front of the bank.

"Stand down. I repeat, stand down now!" she yelled out but was ignored.

Just then, a SWAT team officer yanked opened the door, and there stood a pregnant Debra with her hands raised in fear.

"It's another hostage. Put your guns down now," Dominguez stated, relieved.

Her relief was short lived, however. Two FBI agents waited until Debra was escorted from the front of the bank before they decided to move inside with their weapons drawn, completely ignoring Dominguez's orders. Before Dominguez could make her way inside, shots rang out.

"*I would trade my life for yours. Behind closed doors, everything I'm asking for...*"*-Tupac*

CHAPTER

TEN

G-Easy featuring Halsey — *Him & I*
"See, that's my down bitch, that's my solider... She keep that thang thang if anyone goes there..."

Shawn picked up the iPhone and looked at the screen. His eyes went wide as he watched the two FBI agents pull open the door and rush in. He dropped the phone and removed his gun from his waist as he turned and raced toward DJ, who was putting the steel pipe back in place. "Move!" he yelled out to her, his heart racing a marathon in his chest. If something happened to her, Shawn was going to murder everybody. He slammed into her, pulling her close to his body, shielding them behind the wall, causing her to drop the pipe. With no other choice, Shawn aimed through the bottom half of the glass and opened fire. *BOOM! BOOM! BOOM! BOOM!* The loud blast from the pistol was deafening and was met by bullets from the agents. *POP! POP! POP!*

DJ closed her eyes tight, burying her face in her husband's chest momentarily before pulling Shawn's other gun out of his waistband and contributing to the shootout. *BOOM! BOOM! BOOM!* They could hear the agents retreating and stood completely still, hearts pounding.

"Go by the desk and if they come in, run into the vault," Shawn whispered in her ear.

DJ swiftly moved as Shawn held his position, stealing glances through the broken glass. Once he saw that the coast was clear, he jogged over to a desk, flipping it over on its side before pushing it over to cover the bottom half of the door in order to prevent the cops from looking inside. Shawn backed away, gun gripped in his hand, ready to throw more shots.

He knew they were becoming impatient, but he hadn't expected the ambush. He walked over to DJ and embraced her, securing her in his arms. They had to make it out. He just needed all the pawns on his chess board to make the moves he needed them to make. The iPhone pinged with a notification, and he reluctantly let DJ go to pick up the phone from the ground. He was grateful that it hadn't broken but upset that the FaceTime had ended. Shawn smiled at the two word message that came through the text free app. Now, all he needed was for the cops to have a little bit more patience.

———

"Thank you," Erica said as she passed the female in front of her back her phone. She wiped sweaty palms on the legs of her jeans then stood up and slightly lifted her sweater and shirt. Erica pulled off the duct tape, removing the stack of money that had been inconspicuously secured around her torso.

"It's fifty thousand." She stacked her money on the coffee table and looked up at the female, catching the gleam in her eyes. A smile played at the corner of Erica's lips. "Are you in or not?"

Shameeka stared at the money hungrily. There was no way she was passing up the opportunity to make a tax free fifty bands, especially when it was sitting in front of her face in cash.

"I'm with it," she stated as she grabbed the money, already spending it in her head. This would be the easiest money she ever made.

———

Detective Dominguez paced back-and-forth, fuming at the FBI agents' failed attempt. They had made a split-second decision with no formal warning to the NYPD and had put the reminding hostages deeper in danger; Dominguez was not cool with that.

"How were they able to do that with no repercussions?" Lieutenant Lutrell shook his head, equally upset.

"They feel more superior than us, so they make their moves and shrug us off if we have anything to say about it. But I called and told the chief, and I'm sure they won't try anymore BS unless we're trying it first." He rubbed the back of his neck, overwhelmed. "We need to get this thing over with."

"Umm, I don't mean to interrupt, but Dominguez, you might want to come speak to Debra Chisum asap," her partner stated with an expression that contained glee.

Detective Dominguez's brow bent as she followed.

"Hey, Dominguez," a uniformed officer called out to her, causing her to stop and turn.

"Hey, there's a woman out here saying she has some information for us, and believe me, you wanna hear what she has to say."

———

Shawn looked from face to face of the eight remaining hostages and could see them all in agreement with his proposition.

"So, ya with that? $50,000 for all of ya, wrapped around ya body, and all ya have to do is don't identify my wife when she leaves with ya. She walks out like she's just another hostage. Ya lose nothing but gain $50,000." He let his words sink in. "My intention was never to hurt ya in any way. I just wanted to get the money, so I could get my family everything that they wanted. I'm man enough to accept my consequences, but I need my wife to make it home to our kids," he said sincerely, and from the looks on the hostages' faces, they respected it.

"Yo, cuzzo," Leigh spoke up. "I'm sorry. This shit is my fault, and I really did fuck up. I agree to the $50,000. She wasn't involved." Everybody looked at Leigh with their faces twisted and contempt at the audacity. "You doing a stand-up thing, and I respect you for that."

Shawn nodded, biting down on the inside of his cheek to keep his composure.

"You my family. How can I not forgive you?" Shawn stated as he deadpanned on Leigh. "I also need you to do something for me. Since you family, I only trust you to do it."

Shawn nodded for Leigh to follow him out the vault, giving DJ a wink as he passed her. They walked into the open area, and Shawn tossed DJ's Glock 17 to Leigh who caught it in his hands then dropped it.

"What the fuck?!" Leigh took a step back. The tremor in his voice didn't go unnoticed as his eyes bounced around the room nervously. "What are you doing?"

Shawn walked up on him, this time his two chrome 9mms in his hands and forced them into Leigh's hands before backing away and getting down on his knees with his hands raised in surrender.

"I want you to kill me, cuzzo," Shawn told him as he looked up at Leigh. He observed as the shock plastered on Leigh's face transformed to a look of power as he gripped the two weapons in his hands and aimed them at Shawn.

DJ slowly backpedaled, conflicted. Shawn had told her to trust him, but seeing her husband in that vulnerable position caused anger to ignite in her chest. She made her way into the vault and passed Carrie her cell phone. Carrie took the phone, slightly confused.

"Tuck the phone between your breasts," DJ instructed her. "Ya heard what my husband said. Now I need ya to listen to me. That man is the best man I know —_best husband, father, and provider. I need him, and my kids need him," DJ expressed emotionally. "So, I need ya, and I got another $50,000 for you."

Leigh's heart felt like it would leap out of his chest as he pointed the guns at Shawn. He wasn't a killer, but the thought of how much extra money he could take forced him to squeeze the trigger.

Detective Dominguez finished her notes then turned to the board where she had her information posted.

"This is our suspect." She pointed at the picture on the board. "We have two hostages positively identifying him, DNA evidence on a hostage's sweater, and text messages with his girlfriend."

Dominguez knew she had enough to convict the suspect for the bank burglary and murder of the security guard, but she couldn't do anything without having him in custody. Her head pounded as her mind raced a mile a minute, trying to formulate a plan that would free the hostages safely and apprehend the suspect without incident. The Feds were applying additional pressure and were more than eager to storm in, guns blazing at the man that took shots at federal agents. The safe return of two hostages had brought Dominguez more time, but she didn't know if it was enough. The two women had provided helpful information; it was just the matter of saving the hostages that were still inside the bank. She stopped and stared at the board and couldn't figure out a strategic approach. It was either wait for him to let the hostages go or go in after him and risk the hostages' lives. With a crowd appearing and news cameras rolling, they had to be real careful of how they played things.

"How can I get him to surrender?" she asked herself quietly.

He had already killed a man and busted bullets at law enforcement, proving he was all for the gunplay. Detective Dominguez had to try to speak some compassion into the suspect. Dominguez walked over to the table and picked up the phone, calling the bank. Just like the last few attempts, the phone went unanswered. Worry was beginning to grow in her chest, and she contemplated whether she was making the right decision by milking the clock. She slammed the phone down and let out a breath of exasperation, pressing her palms to the table. Her career meant everything to her, and with already negotiating to release the two hostages on her first job as the negotiator, she would receive praise whether the suspect was brought in dead or alive. The remaining hostages would be considered casualties, but Dominguez's good heart outweighed any praise or promotion.

"How do I get them all out?" she questioned herself.

The suspect knew there was absolutely no way out as a free man, but Dominguez couldn't understand why he was prolonging the inevitable.

"What does he have under his sleeve?"

"Figure it out yet?" Lieutenant Lutrell asked. He could see how conflicted Dominguez was about the situation. She had never been one to wear a good poker face when it came to victims in any case. She usually wore her heart on her sleeve, and it was what made her a good detective, but sometimes, he needed her to control the emotions and think logically. It was what would make her a great detective. Dominguez shook her head no, her shoulders slumped in defeat.

"We got him. He's identified, and there's no way out of this, but I won't be able to live with myself if another hostage is murdered when I could have prevented it."

"You can't save everybody," Lieutenant Lutrell stated seriously. "Sometimes, there's gonna be victims who meet their demise. It's just how life works, but the ones you do save should help you sleep a little better at night."

Dominguez took his words in, but before she could respond, she heard a loud pop, then an officer was reporting the sound of a gunshot.

"*C*ross my heart, hope to die. To you, I've never lied. For you, I'd take a life. It's him and I, and I swear... 'Til the end, I'ma ride wit' you..." -Halsey*

EPILOGUE

Fabulous featuring Chris Brown & Teyana Taylor - *Us Vs The World*

"For better, for worse (worse), until death do us part (yeah). You started with a canvas (ooh) and we turned it to some art (oh yeah)..."

Two Days Later...

Christmas Eve...

Detective Dominguez sipped her matcha latte as she went through the case file that was perched against her steering wheel. She took a sip then placed the drink in the cup holder before she reached into her skintight jean pocket and removed her vape pen then focused back on the file in front of her. Dominguez really didn't know what she was doing on Christmas Eve, sitting in her car in front of the Maspeth Federal Savings Bank, looking through the file of a closed case. The case was labeled solved, but she couldn't shake the feeling that there was a lot more to it. The bank heist had ended minutes after the reporting of a shot going off with the suspect dead, killed by the remaining security guard's licensed firearm, a justified homicide. Soon after, the doors were pulled opened, and the remaining hostages rushed out, quickly being brought to safety. They had all been physically fine and escorted home where they would be spending the holidays with their family after their traumatic experience. Dominguez's heart warmed at the thought, but her mind was bombarded with suspicion, even today on a breezy Christmas Eve, a day she had used vacation time to get off; she couldn't get her mind off the bank heist.

The evidence was all foolproof and would have convicted the suspect beyond a reasonable doubt, but Detective Dominguez had always been the type of woman who would listen to what was said and heard what wasn't. She took a deep pull of the vape, sending smoke into her lungs, before her full lips puckered and then slowly blew out the smoke, hoping to release some of the thoughts consuming her mind. Dominguez looked at every piece of evidence, trying to spot anything she might have missed. There was a photo taken by one of the bank tellers, Carrie Davis, of the suspect holding a hostage at gunpoint. There was a description of the suspect given by the first released hostage, Erica Porter. The suspect's blood was on the sweater of the second released hostage, Debra Chisum. All three weapons used during the heist, including the gun used to murder the security guard, Elliot Brinks, had the suspect's fingerprints, and the icing on the cake was the testimony provided by the suspect's girlfriend, Shameeka Watts. Shameeka had stated that the suspect informed her of his plan and tried to involve her along with an unknown friend of his. Shameeka had even been able to provide a description of the stolen vehicle she had last seen him in, which the police had found up the block.

Detective Dominguez leaned her head back, questions nobody else seemed to ask bouncing around her head. She never understood why Erica Porter had been the first hostage released instead of one of the two pregnant women or the man who had epilepsy. Dominguez questioned how the 1.8 million had walked out the door undetected or why the suspect used one gun to kill the security guard but two others to shoot at the federal agents. She hadn't missed the fact that the lifeless male suspect wore a female turtleneck under his hoodie or that two out of the eleven hostages were not seen on video surveillance footage before the cameras were smashed, but the suspect had entered approximately seven minutes earlier. The suspect's bruised torso and busted lips also raised questions but was accepted as results of a tussle with a hostage defending his wife. Everybody just wanted to put the bank heist behind them and celebrate the holidays, but Dominguez wanted answers. It was the only way she would be able to put it out her mind.

Dominguez closed the file and stuffed it in her purse before bringing her engine to life. She was already late for the holiday get together she had agreed to attend. She ran her hand through her long hair as she looked down at her clothes; the tight jeans, Doc Martens, and sweater would have to do. She looked toward the bank one last time, and goosebumps formed on her arms as her heartbeat rapidly increased, and her instincts kicked in.

"That's one of the hostages," she recalled.

She watched him walk into the narrow alleyway where the dumpster was, only to return with a large garbage bag. He threw the bag in the trunk of his car then walked over to the driver's side and climbed in. "He is the mastermind," Dominguez said with certainty as she pulled out right behind him, keeping a good distance, so he wouldn't spot her. As she trailed him, Dominguez thought back to her interaction with the man. He had a strong presence, an air of confidence and a demeanor that was too cool for school. Seeing him now brought on the feeling that he was the suspect the entire time. Then, the full picture came together.

"His wife was involved too."

———

The cocky smile that was plastered on Shawn's face couldn't be contained as he pushed the Bentley down the avenue with close to a million dollars in the trunk. He was enroute to the Poconos where his family had been since the previous day. The plan was to spend the holidays amongst some good friends at the cozy cabin, but the day after the ball dropped, they were loading up the newly purchased 2016 Benz Sprinter, putting the past behind them, and moving far away where nobody could find them. With more than $850,000, they were ready to live their best lives, and Shawn couldn't wait. Shawn looked in the rearview mirror at the backseat that was packed with boxes on top of boxes of Christmas gifts, and he smiled. Everything that had been on the kids' wish list to Santa Claus was purchased, minus the flying unicorn, and unbeknownst to his wife, he had closed the deal on the house she had fallen in love with. This was a holiday for the history books, and if he had to do it all again to be rewarded with the smiles and hugs he would receive, he would do it again in a New York minute. Shawn reflected on the bank heist and let out a chuckle. "You really him," he said to himself in praise as he thought back to the final moments in the bank.

Shawn looked at Leigh as he repeatedly pulled the trigger, his forehead wrinkled in utter confusion that bullets weren't penetrating Shawn's body. Shawn couldn't help but to laugh as he stood from his knees, eyes piercing Leigh.

"You really think I'll let your bitch ass take my life?" he asked with a shake of his head.

The clips had been emptied, and Leigh had played right into Shawn's hand. Shawn had used his gloved hands to toss Leigh DJ's gun that had killed the security guard, causing Leigh to leave his fingerprints on the murder weapon. Then, Shawn had forced his two chrome 9mms that were used to shoot at the federal agents into Leigh's hands to leave fingerprints on those as well. The second Shawn had got down on his knees and raised his hand in surrender, Leigh had aimed the guns at him, unknowingly for the picture DJ was snapping on Carrie's phone.

Maybe if Leigh knew that Erica had described him as a suspect, that Dehra had confirmed it and provided her sweater that he had left his blood on while leaning on her, and that Shameeka had told the detectives on the case that he had mentioned his plan to rob the bank, he would have moved a little smarter. While Shawn taunted him, DJ was inside the vault, assisting the hostages with wrapping $100K around their torsos. It was their reward for pointing the finger at Leigh and turning a blind eye to the couple's involvement —a token for their silence that they had accepted without any hesitation. While helping the security guard, DJ made him an offer that even Shawn was unaware about.

"I got an extra $100,000 if you kill him," DJ whispered to the security guard.

The guard's greed could be seen through his eyes. It was more money than he would see working for the next year. DJ inconspicu-

ously passed him his licensed pistol and stood on her tiptoes to speak in his ear.

"I'm sorry for your partner. I was just trying to save my husband's life. Please forgive us but just know if it wasn't for Leigh, we wouldn't have done this."

Shawn shook his head at Leigh in disgust.

"I came to you for help cause you were supposed to be family," he said as he peeped the security guard creeping toward them from behind Leigh. Shawn's eyes went to the gun in the guard's hands before looking in Leigh's eyes.

"Thank you for the motivation to hit this lick. My family's straight now."

BOOM!

He watched as the guard put a bullet in Leigh's back. Leigh's body fell forward, dead before he hit the ground. Shawn locked eyes with the security guard, and they exchanged a nod of understanding. He knew the next few minutes were the most important, so Shawn raced over to his wife.

"Don't leave your gloves anywhere, stuff them in your panties," he told her as he passed her his.

He then grabbed the four buckets of KFC the chicken had come in. They were now stuffed to the top with stacks of unmarked bills. Shawn made sure nobody was paying attention before placing the buckets at the bottom of a garbage bag and covering it with papers. He said a silent prayer before moving back toward his wife. This was the moment of truth. Between both of them, they had $250,000 secured to their body, which was enough money to move on with their lives. All they had to do was get through the next hour of investigation, then they were free. Shawn knew he would be returning for the buckets of money, but even if it wasn't there when he doubled back, he was satisfied with the earnings. He held his wife's hand and kissed her lips as he looked over at the hostages, who all gave him *head nods and smiles of assurance. They had his back, and all he had to do was lead the way out the bank.*

"Let's go home to our kids, beautiful."

They simultaneously walked out the door, and the rest was history. They had made it home and spent the rest of the day with the kids and the rest of the night fucking until the sun came up. The next day, Shawn was out and about, buying everything the kids wanted plus more. They had already decided that they were kissing New York goodbye, so Shawn made a purchase of a house in West Virginia that DJ had fallen in love with. Upon returning to New York, retrieving money from the dumpster was his first stop, and luckily, it was all there.

Shawn rode through traffic, his head bopping to the music and his heart warm. He couldn't wait to see his wife and the little ones' faces when they opened their presents. That was going to be the best gift he got besides the news of his wife's pregnancy.

Shawn took the exit to the Poconos, fully aware of the car trailing behind him. He was too cautious to be caught slipping and had peeped the female detective the second after he pulled away from the bank. She had seen him stuff the bag in the trunk, so if her intentions were to detain him, she would have pulled him over about two hours ago. It made no sense to take on a high-speed chase or jump to conclusions. He had ignored the impulse and decided to see how things played out, so he remained calm, leading her to the rented cabin. They both pulled into the driveway and killed their engines. His wife and kids were inside, so he wouldn't turn his Christmas Eve into the Fourth of July, but there was also no way he was allowing her to take him away from them. Shawn took a deep breath as he removed the pistol that was in his stash spot and tucked it in his waistband. If the detective didn't come correct, the .45 ACP was going to be introduced to her.

Shawn stepped out, eyes locked on Detective Dominguez as she climbed out her car and slammed her door shut before taking a few steps forward until they were at arm's reach. They stared at each other in silence for a few seconds before Shawn spoke.

"How we gonna do this?" he asked her, observing her. No guns or badges were on display; that had to be a good sign.

Detective Dominguez didn't know how to answer that question. Her heart pounded in her chest as she cleared the lump that had formed in her throat. They both knew the deal, so there was no point in beating around the bush.

"I just wanna know why did you and your wife do it and how did ya pull it off." A hint of fascination could be detected in her voice. The couple had succeeded in an intricate situation, and Dominguez couldn't help but to be intrigued. She wouldn't prosecute them, but she wanted answers to her questions. She crossed her arms over her chest as she awaited his answers.

Shawn chuckled. The detective was wasting both their time if she thought he would verbally admit or explain anything. Before he could reply, the door to the cabin opened, and his five-year-old stepdaughter ran out. Amber pounced at him excitably, laughing joyously as he picked her up and kissed her forehead.

"Shawn!" She showed him the gold bracelet with the unicorn charm on her wrist before hugging his neck tightly. "We missed you. We can't open more gifts without you."

Shawn turned his attention back to Dominguez as DJ walked out the cabin and made her way toward them.

"You got your answer to one question," he responded as he held Amber.

DJ wrapped her arm around her husband's waist, and she leaned into his body, eyes on Dominguez.

"Princess, go inside to your brother."

They watched as she climbed down and ran back inside.

"She's my present?" DJ asked Shawn, raising her eyebrow suggestively as her eyes roamed the detective's frame.

Dominguez felt her face flush as she stood in front of the couple. She couldn't deny that she held a level of respect for them, and Shawn making the motive clear was admirable. They had done it for their family. They had risked their lives in order to give their kids a great Christmas and foundation. Movement by the front door caught Dominguez's attention, and her eyes grew wide in shock when the nine hostages from the bank stepped onto the porch of the cabin. She nodded slowly then looked back at Shawn and DJ, her respect for them increasing.

"The case is closed; the suspect is dead."

"You followed me for a reason," Shawn responded.

"I'm curious by nature. Something told me since the moment I interviewed ya two that ya couldn't just be hostages," Dominguez stated.

She had felt their aura from the gate. Something about them told her they were too smart for their own good. Clearly, she was right.

"You ain't follow me for two hours just to clear your curious mind," Shawn pressed, baiting her.

"$50,000," Dominguez blurted out, surprising herself.

Shawn nodded slowly then looked at DJ, who was looking up at him. They shared a smirk, silently exchanging praises. They had hit a lick for the holiday that would set them up for life, gave the kids everything they wanted, and got away with it.

"We got $50,000 for you," DJ agreed to Dominguez's

request. "But you have to be our Christmas present." She allowed her eyes to take in the detective again.

Lori Dominguez was a very attractive woman with authority, and tonight, DJ wanted to dominate her. She held out her manicured hand toward Dominguez. After a few beats, Dominguez reached out, placing her hand in DJ's and followed them inside. This was a holiday that they would never forget.

"*Mobbin' with you for the family, put a job in with you. I want all of your love, hope that's not a problem with you...*" *-Fabulous*

The End

Did you enjoy the read?
Let us know how much by leaving us a review on Amazon and Goodreads.

OTHER BOOKS BY

URBAN AINT DEAD

Tales 4rm Da Dale

The Hottest Summer Ever

Hittin' Licks For The Holidays: Atlanta

Wet Dreams On Lockdown: The Nurse

How To Publish A Book From Prison

By **Elijah R. Freeman**

Despite The Odds

By **Juhnell Morgan**

Good Girls Gone Rogue

Good Girls Gone Rogue 2

By **Manny Black**

Hittaz

Hittaz 2

Hittaz 3

Hittaz 4

Hittaz 5

Coldhearted

Coldhearted 2

Coldhearted 3

By **Lou Garden Price, Sr.**

Charge It To The Game

Charge It To The Game 2

A Summer To Remember With My Hitta

Snatched Up By A Hitta

Santa Sent Me A Real One For Christmas

Wet Dreams On Lockdown: The Unit Manager

Thug Me The Right Way 2

Thug Me The Right Way 3

Seizing A Gangsta's Heart For The Summer

Yours For The Taking

By **Nai**

A Set Up For Revenge

A Set Up For Revenge 2

Wet Dreams On Lockdown: The Librarian

By **Ashley Williams**

Trickin' On A Heaux For Christmas

Homie Hoppin' For The Holidays

Wet Dreams On Lockdown: The Female C.O

Letters Of His Love

By **Telia Teanna**

The State's Witness

The State's Witness 2

The State's Witness 3

This Time Won't You Save Me

This Time Won't You Save Me 2

His Summer Side Piece

By **Kyiris Ashley**

Stuck In The Trenches

Stuck In The Trenches 2

By **Huff Tha Great**

The Swipe

The Swipe 2

By **Toōla**

Melted The Heart Of a Menace

Wet Dreams On Lockdown: Lieutenant Grace

By **P. Wise**

Merry Trapmas

By **Mia Sky**

Thug Me The Right Way

By **DiamondATL & Nai**

Wet Dreams On Lockdown: The Counselor

By **Paris Iman**

Wet Dreams On Lockdown: The Male C.O

By **Tamyra Griffin**

Wet Dreams On Lockdown: The Captain

By **TN Jones**

Wet Dreams On Lockdown: The Warden

By **Shawnice**

Atlantastan

Atlantastan 2

By **Chris Green**

IN The Streetz

IN The Streetz 2

IN The Streetz 3

By **Tron Hill**

Coming Soon From
URBAN AINT DEAD

The Hottest Summer Ever 2
THE G-CODE
Tales 4rm Da Dale 2
How To Invest In The Stock Market From Prison
By **Elijah R. Freeman**

Hittaz 6
By **Lou Garden Price, Sr.**

Good Girls Gone Rogue 3
By **Manny Black**

Despite The Odds 2
By **Juhnell Morgan**

The Swipe 3
By **Toōla**

Charge It To The Game 3
Wrapped Up In A Hitta's Love For Christmas
By **Nai**

This Time Won't You Save Me 3
Healing The Heart Of A Detroit Gangsta
A Holiday Heist
By **Kyiris Ashley**

Atlantastan 3
By **Chris Green**

IN The Streetz 4
By **Tron Hill**

BOOKS BY
URBAN AINT DEAD'S C.E.O

<u>Elijah R. Freeman</u>

Triggadale 1, 2 & 3

Tales 4rm Da Dale

The Hottest Summer Ever

Murda Was The Case 1, 2 & 3

Hittin' Licks For The Holidays: Atlanta

Wet Dreams On Lockdown: The Nurse

How To Publish A Book From Prison

STAY CONNECTED

Follow
Elijah R. Freeman
On Social Media
FB: Elijah R. Freeman
IG: @the_future_of_urban_fiction